THE CASE OF THE DRAGON IN DISTRESS

The Case of the Dragon in Distress

A McGurk Fantasy

BY E. W. HILDICK

Macmillan Publishing Company   New York

Collier Macmillan Canada   Toronto

Maxwell Macmillan International Publishing Group
New York   Oxford   Singapore   Sydney

Macmillan Publishing Company
866 Third Avenue, New York, NY 10022
Collier Macmillan Canada, Inc.
1200 Eglinton Avenue East, Suite 200
Don Mills, Ontario M3C 3N1
First edition
Printed in the United States of America

10   9   8   7   6   5   4   3   2   1

The text of this book is set in 12 point Caledonia.

Library of Congress Cataloging-in-Publication Data
Hildick, E. W. (Edmund Wallace).
The case of the dragon in distress : a McGurk fantasy / by E. W.
Hildick. — 1st ed.
Summary: The McGurk Organization members are transported back to
the twelfth century where they encounter an evil princess who tries
to hold them captive,
ISBN 0-02-743931-3
[1. Time travel—Fiction.   2. Knights and knighthood—Fiction.
3. Middle Ages—Fiction.]   I. Title.
PZ7.H5463Casd   1991
[Fic]—dc20   90-13538

Contents

1 The Black Boxes

How did the McGurk Organization get to be held captive in a castle dungeon? A *real* castle? A *real* dungeon? In real chains, with real executioners? Men with black hoods and short black tunics and long black hose ending in pointed shoes? Men with orders to put us slowly to death, one by one—and to do this as soon as they were given the command by their boss, one of the most ruthless rulers ever?

I tell you, we've been in some pretty tight spots in our time, but never one as tight as this.

It all started—well, some of us think it started with Brains Bellingham's black boxes. It couldn't have happened without them, that's for sure. But personally I think it started before then. I mean I don't believe it would have happened the way it did, if it hadn't been for that old round table with which McGurk replaced the oblong one in his basement, our headquarters.

After all, that was what got us all thinking about King Arthur and *his* round table and knights and stuff. We even designed shields for ourselves like *we* were a bunch of knights and highborn ladies. I mentioned this in my record of *The Case of the Purloined Parrot*. Here are copies of those shields, with the designs telling about our strong points or main features:

Joey Rockaway

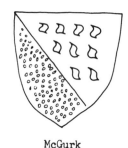

McGurk

Wanda Grieg

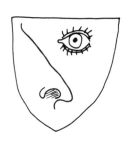

Willie Sandowsky

Brains Bellingham

Mari Yoshimura

Ms. Ellis at school got to hear of this.

"What a good idea!" she said. "The Age of Chivalry. We'll make that our topic in history for the next few weeks. And we'll start by designing shields like this for every one of us. Then we'll make models of castles, and draw pictures of how they dressed in those days, and . . ."

And so on.

Models, pictures, written descriptions, little playlets, even a special code of gallant and courteous conduct for the guys to uphold in all their dealings with the girls. You know what some teachers are like when they get hooked on an idea like this.

Then again, maybe something else triggered our adventure. Like one of those role-playing fantasy games some of us had been messing with. Monsters and Mazes, for example.

"That's definitely what started it!" moaned Willie Sandowsky at our darkest hour, chained up in that evil-smelling dungeon. "If it hadn't been for that game, we'd never have gotten into this."

He spoke with deep feeling. I mean, with his sensitive nose, just the smell of that damp dark hole was torture enough.

McGurk himself had his own theory.

"Your black boxes, Officer Bellingham," he said. "They're what got us *here*. But it might have been someplace different if we hadn't all watched that

Dracula movie last Saturday."

There was something in that, too. The drinking of human blood *was* one of the chief motives in this case. And the fact that it was McGurk's blood the evil owner of that castle was especially keen on sampling—well, that naturally helped him to make up his mind, I guess.

"If you ask *me*, it all started long before we were even born," said Wanda Grieg. "More than eight centuries ago and four thousand miles away."

"Yes," said Mari Yoshimura. "Around the year eleven seventy-five. Somewhere in the wild hill country on the Welsh border with England."

Those two had been listening to Ms. Ellis's lessons very carefully. After all, they'd had the time. We guys were kept too busy being polite and courteous toward them to take in *every* fact.

Anyway, that's enough about why it happened the way it did. Here's how and when it actually started.

It was one Tuesday morning during the first week of the summer vacation. McGurk had been getting kind of antsy. The usual reason. Not having a case to work on.

Willie and I were late. We'd been working out new rules for Monsters and Mazes—rules that would speed up the action a little. It isn't an easy game with just two persons, and none of the others had shown much interest.

"You're late!" said McGurk, scowling at us through the cloud of bunched-up freckles that surrounded his eyes.

He was sitting in his usual rocking chair. (Oh, yes! The idea of the round table was that no one would be sitting at the head or the bottom. Everyone would be equal. But when one of the group has a big rocking chair and all the rest have ordinary hard-backed chairs—well, I don't think King Arthur would have approved of that. And I'm *certain* Sir Galahad and Sir Lancelot and the other knights wouldn't have.)

"Sorry," I said, "we were just—"

"Wasting time on that dumb role-playing game," he said. "I'm surprised at *you*, Officer Rockaway. And you, Officer Sandowsky."

Wanda Grieg gave her long yellow hair a sassy sort of toss and nudged Mari Yoshimura.

"Look who's calling role-playing games dumb!" she said.

"Well, so they are, Officer Grieg," said McGurk.

"Coming from you, McGurk, that's a laugh," said Wanda. "Why, you're *always* playing a role."

"Me?"

"Yes, you! Playing the role of the head of a detective organization."

McGurk's green eyes widened.

"Well, so I *am* head of a detective organization! That's no role! That's for real!"

Wanda shrugged.

"Have it your own way, McGurk. But what's the use of a detective organization without any case?"

"That's what this meeting's about," said McGurk. "I was hoping one of you might have heard of something."

He glared at us one at a time, but we only shook our heads.

"Maybe," said Mari, "maybe Brains has heard of a case. Maybe that's why he's late."

McGurk grunted.

"Fat chance! The last I heard from him, he was all set to work on some old electronic apparatus his uncle's given him."

"Well, he *is* our science expert," I said. "Perhaps it's something we could use in our detective work."

"Yeah!" said Willie. "Like some special bugging device."

"Or a machine for recording voiceprints," said Mari.

McGurk began to look a little less annoyed.

"Well, if he doesn't come soon—"

"Hi, guys!" said Brains, bursting into the room. "Wait till I tell you what I've got here!"

What he'd got there made him look like one of those photography nuts with thousands of things hanging from straps on both shoulders. Or correction: like some sort of state-of-the-art maypole, the way those straps were swinging around as he bustled to his seat.

Then, when he was at rest and putting the things on the table, I saw they were flat black boxes with steel rods poking out of some of them.

"Walkie-talkies," I said.

"Yeah," murmured McGurk, eagerly reaching out for one. "Six of them."

"To give them their real name," said Brains, casting me a cocky look, "they're two-way, portable, battery-operated transmitting/receiving sets."

McGurk was getting to look very interested as he pulled out the antenna on the one he was holding.

"For us?" he said. "For the Organization?"

"Yes—one each—sure," said Brains. He was starting to look a bit embarrassed. His face was turning red, and the red kept on creeping above his ears and even started showing through his short, fair, bristly hair. Another sign was the trapped look in his eyes as they began to roll from side to side behind his thick glasses.

"Well, I've switched it on," said McGurk. "And sure enough there's a hum. What next? Suppose I want to send a message?"

"You—you turn the top switch up," stammered Brains. "Up for sending, down for receiving. But—"

"Okay," said McGurk, turning up the top switch. "Now you set yours to the receive position."

"It's already set there," said Brains. "But—"

"Okay, then." McGurk rocked back in his chair, holding the instrument close to his mouth, looking pleased. "Now hear this! Calling all officers of the McGurk Organization. This is your chief speaking. Mayday, Mayday, Mayday! The perpetrators have surrounded me! They're moving in! Get here quick! Lights and sirens all the way! They're . . ."

He trailed off.

"What's wrong?" he said. "Haven't I got it tuned in or something?"

"I keep trying to *tell* you, McGurk!" said Brains, his face redder than ever. "They all work on the same special fixed frequency, which makes them just right for us. I made sure of that when Uncle Chuck gave them to me. He got them in a fire sale and—"

"We don't want their history, Officer Bellingham," said McGurk, scowling. "How come my message isn't being picked up? I coulda been shot to ribbons by now!"

"That's what I keep trying to explain, McGurk!" said Brains. "There's nothing wrong with them. They were giving a very faint signal at first, but I soon fixed that."

"You could have fooled me," I said, putting one

of them close to my ear. "Go on, McGurk," I said.
"Say again."

"Calling all officers of the McGurk Organization,"
he began. "Mayday, May—"

I was shaking my head.

"Not a cheep."

"Is it switched on right?" said Willie.

"Yes," I said, "but—"

"Will you *please* listen to me!" yelled Brains, slap-
ping the table and making some of the straps writhe
like snakes. "What I'm trying to tell you all is that
somehow—when I was fixing them to give louder
signals—I must have done something else."

"*What* something else?" growled McGurk, his
eyes now just two green slits in the bunched-up
freckles.

Brains was sweating.

"Like they work perfectly," he said. "But only at
night. After dark. I guess it has something to do
with the Appleton layer—the—the ionosphere—"

"Never mind the technical details, Officer Bellingham. You mean they really do work? You tested
them?"

"Yes. They work fine. But only after dark."

McGurk's eyes were beginning to glow.

"So what?" he said. "That makes them *perfect* for
the Organization! Now we can keep in touch with
each other after we've gone to bed! In complete

confidence!" His whole face was glowing now. His red hair seemed to have gone half a dozen shades brighter. "It makes us a twenty-four-hour-a-day Organization!"

"Yes," I said, getting enthusiastic myself. "With a new slogan: The McGurk Organization Never Sleeps!"

"Oh, boy!" murmured Wanda, pulling a face.

But she was just as eager as the rest of us when McGurk handed us one each and said we'd give them a try that very night.

Well . . . I don't usually like saying, "Little did we know," because it's such a tired old phrase. But really, I mean, little *did* we know, any of us, just what a stupendous, mind-blowing, nightmarish situation those little old black boxes were going to land us in!

2 In the Cavern

As soon as I got into bed that evening, I began to try to get in touch with the others.

"Do you read me?" I said. "Over."

There was no reply. Just a faint hiss.

"Do you read me?" I repeated. "Over."

Again no reply.

I repeated the message five or six more times. Same result.

So then I decided to vary it.

"Are you reading me? Over."

And I repeated this one five or six times.

Nothing.

I was beginning to wonder if I'd been unlucky and drawn a defective set. I had visions of the others all chatting away, with McGurk fussing about why I wasn't joining in.

Then again, I thought, maybe none of them had had any better luck. Maybe all the sets were defective. Or could it be that it wasn't dark enough yet?

It seemed it to me. The only light was coming

11

from neighboring houses, creating a glow behind the drapes and sharper glints at the edges.

"Read me, do you?" I said, trying another variation. "Over."

Then I tried, "Reading me, are you?" and "Me, do you read?" and "Me, Joey, do you read?" and "Me, Joey, are you reading?"

The reason I kept trying was that when I pressed the switch to receive I could just hear faint whispering scratchy voices. Like you hear on the phone sometimes, when you get a bad line. I couldn't recognize any of them. They were too distorted. I couldn't even recognize Willie's, who only lives next door and who you might have expected to come in clearest. And not only couldn't I recognize the voices, I couldn't make out any of the words, either. Except one. "*Eftsoons.*" That came through clear enough. I might not have recognized even that, it was so strange. But it was one of the list I'd made of words used in the Age of Chivalry. Ms. Ellis had given me an A for that list. . . .

I guess I must have been nodding off by this time. It was getting late. Soon afterward, I did drop off—completely.

I must have fallen pretty fast asleep, because when I woke up it was pitch-dark. The neighbors must have switched their lights off and gone to bed, because now there was no glow coming from behind the drapes. I turned my head and no—there wasn't even the chink of light that had been coming from under the bedroom door.

I reached out to where I knew the lamp was, on the bedside table beside the walkie-talkie set. I felt nothing. I stretched my arm out farther—and then drew it back quickly.

My hand had scraped against something hard. Rock hard. In fact it *was* rock, as I soon discovered when I began to feel around gingerly. Craggy, jagged, damp rock. Also cold. Very cold.

I sat up sharp, shivering.

It was still pitch-dark.

But—*rock?* In my bedroom?

Then I realized I was not only feeling it with my hand. Under me it was hard, too. I patted around at the sides of my legs. Where were the sheets and the other bed covers? Where was the bed itself?

One of my hands knocked against something else hard. But this was smooth and small. The black box.

But forget the box, I told myself. What's this *straw* doing here?

That's what it felt like.

Straw.

What was I doing, lying on hard, damp, cold rock on some kind of straw bed? Where was my real bed? What *was* this? What was going *on*, for Pete's sake?

My hand came in contact with the set again. I got

hold of it and held it near my face. And yes—although I couldn't see it even that close, I could feel its outlines and the strap. Also it was faintly humming. I fumbled for the switch and pressed it up.

"M-m-may—!"

I took a deep breath. The word had come out in a stuttering bleat, like a lost lamb's. A very frightened lost lamb's. I cleared my throat.

"Mayday!" I said. "Mayday, Mayday, Mayday! Willie, Brains—any of you—please come in if you read me!"

I pressed the switch. There was a distinct change of tone in the hum. I thought I could hear someone breathing. I crossed the fingers of my free hand.

Then I heard The Voice.

"You are in a strange new environment," it said. "At least it is new to you." A man's voice, deep and grave and unhurried. "Actually it is an old, old environment. An old, old environment bristling with dangers—with pitfalls and traps and evildoers and monsters beyond your wildest nightmares. Have a care!"

It didn't seem to be coming from the set at all, once it had gotten into its stride. It seemed to be coming from all around, echoing and reechoing from every corner of the room or den or lair or cavern or cell or whatever it was. And it wasn't a voice I recognized.

Unless—

"*Hey!* Mari!" I said accusingly, when it was through. I mean only she, Mari Yoshimura, could have imitated a voice like that, not to mention throwing it so it seemed to come from every which way.

But there was no reply, even when I pressed the switch to transmit and said, "Come on, Mari! Cut it out!"

I opened my eyes, which I'd kept closed tight while trying to recognize the voice. Not that it would have made much difference in *there*.

But not so fast, I told myself, blinking. It didn't seem quite so dark now. It was very dim still, but there did seem to be a faint source of light from farther along the cavern. Enough at any rate to tell that it *was* a cavern.

I got to my feet and went toward it. And sure enough, the closer I went the more I was able to see faint irregular spots and cracks of light, coming from around the edges of what seemed to be, and felt like, a huge boulder.

I tried to move it.

It didn't budge. Not a fraction of an inch.

Then I heard The Voice again.

"What are you doing?"

It came from behind me.

I thought I could make out a darker shadow at

the back, but couldn't be sure.

"What are you doing?" it said again.

"Trying to get out of here," I said.

"Why?"

"To see where I am."

"I told you before. In a strange new environment."

"I know *that*—uh—sir," I added, realizing I'd been sounding a bit mad and that whoever this was he was a much older person than I. Also probably a much more powerful one. "I meant just *where*. Geographically, that is."

"Do you not *know* where?"

"All I know is that this isn't my bedroom at home. And somehow I get the feeling that this isn't even in the U.S.A."

"Is not in where?"

"The U.S.A. America."

"No, child, it is not. You are in the mountains of Wales. America has yet to be discovered. Even if you were to get out of here, you would not see the U—what did you call it?"

"The United States of America."

"Ah!" The strange note of joy in his voice made me jump. "The *United* States! You have just uttered the first magic word!"

"Oh?" I said, not quite liking this talk of magic.

"Yes," The Voice went on. "Only in union, in

united effort, will you get through this ordeal—this adventure—alive."

I swallowed again. There you go, I thought. Ordeal. That's what this was going to be.

"Oh," I said, "uh—really? Well, in that case I only hope that McGurk and the others—"

"Who?"

"Jack McGurk, my friend, and—"

"You have just uttered the second magic word. The name of Sir Jack McGurk, dubbed Knight of the Fiery Freckles. By you yourself, I believe. Well, *he* is here in this land, too. With several other of his retainers. But they are in thrall. Spellbound. They can do nothing until someone comes along and releases them."

"Who?"

"Can you not guess?"

"Me?"

"Forsooth. Surely."

"So how do I get out of here?"

"By uttering the third magic word."

"Which is what? Sir?"

"I cannot tell you. Save to say it is a word as close to you as your very skin."

I thought for a few moments. Then:

"Uh—my *name*? Joey?"

There was suddenly a rumbling and trembling close to me. The huge rock had moved all right, but it was still in place.

Then I had it.

"*I* know," I said. "Rockaway! Joey Rockaway!"

And, sure enough, as it rumbled and trembled again and I began to push, that old rock began to roll slowly away to one side.

3 Statues?

I turned and looked back. Now I could see all the way in there and it *was* a cave. I could see the straw on the floor with my walkie-talkie at the side of it. But there was no sign of anyone else.

Well, here goes, I thought.

I darted in and grabbed the box and darted out again. I needn't have worried, though. Nobody rolled the boulder back in place. Nor did it roll itself back. At least I was free to move on.

I turned to look at the land in front of the cavern. Here is a cross-sectional view of it which I made later:

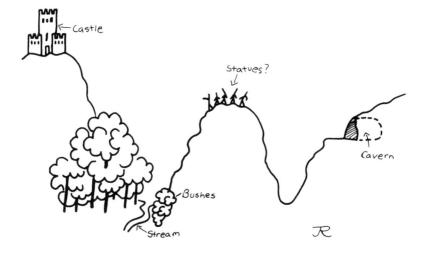

Immediately in front of the cave was a kind of natural platform, on which I was now standing. Then the ground fell away sharply into a ravine strewn with rocks and boulders, and with patches of scrubby grass and a few solitary stunted trees and bushes. At that point, of course, I couldn't see the woods and the stream on the far side of the hill in front of me. Only the castle, towering there in the distance, glowing a ghostly white against the menacing gray sky. Between me and it, on top of the hill across the ravine, there was a group of statues. At least I thought they were statues.

I slung the walkie-talkie over my shoulder, took a deep breath and gave my cap a tug. That last movement made me look down at myself and realize for the first time that I was wearing my regular clothes: T-shirt, jeans, sneakers, and, of course, my Giants cap. This made me feel better. It was pretty raw and chilly even though it was summer, judging from the leaves on the few trees I could see. And although the shirt was on the flimsy side, at least I wasn't in my pajamas and barefooted.

It didn't take me long to scramble down and up the other side to where the figures were. Down at the bottom I lost sight of them for a while, but that didn't bother me much. My main aim was to get up onto that hill and see what lay between there and the castle. So you can imagine my surprise when I reached the top and saw those figures again, much closer. I tell you, I nearly flipped and rolled back to the bottom.

Statues?

Schmatues!

This group was the rest of the McGurk Organization! All looking safe and sound in *their* ordinary clothes—but motionless, like they'd been killed and stuffed and mounted in their characteristic attitudes!

I mean, there was McGurk, scowling at Brains and pointing at the black box slung over Brains's shoulder. (The others had theirs with them, too, I noticed.) And there was Brains looking injured and indignant, his shoulders hunched up and his hands held out from his sides, palms facing McGurk, protesting.

Mari was standing in a similar position, but *her* accuser was Willie, his eyes wide and startled, pointing at her with one hand and rubbing his nose with the other. As for Wanda, she was glaring defiantly at McGurk, with her lip curled and (this was the spookiest thing of all) one wing of her hair frozen motionless in midair, caught in the middle of being tossed.

"Hey! Are you guys all right?"

The sound of my voice seemed to unfreeze them. I remembered what the owner of the mystery voice had said as they all turned to me. This was what he must have meant when he said they were all being held "in thrall."

"Where've *you* been?" were McGurk's welcoming words.

I told him about waking up in the cave and The Voice.

"Yeah," said Willie. "We heard him, too. Through these boxes."

"So now maybe you'll stop accusing Mari of throwing her voice," said Wanda.

"One box, yes, maybe," Mari said to Willie. "But not all five at the same time!"

Now I know Mari very well. She likes to play tricks with her voice, yes. But I also know when she's telling the truth—and she was now.

"So whose voice *is* it?" said Willie.

"The controller," said McGurk, emphatically. "All good time-machine experiments have them. Right, Officer Bellingham?"

"Well . . ." murmured Brains, looking doubtful.

"It stands to reason," said McGurk. "If a time machine can transport you back to another century, it can also fix you up with some kind of guide."

"Like in those role-playing fantasies?" I said.

"Or like a spirit guide," said Wanda. "When they have séances and put you in touch with dead loved ones."

"That's garbage!" said Brains.

"Well, *this* isn't," said McGurk. "This one's for real. I mean we all heard him. Right, men?"

We agreed. Even Brains had to give a grunt of assent.

"Anyway, did *you* hear him telling us about the castle and the dragon and the princess?" Wanda asked me.

"No," I said. "What was all *that* about?"

"Over at the castle," said McGurk. "There's a princess. She's being held prisoner by a dragon."

"Baloney!" said Brains. "There's no such creature. Never was. You heard what Ms. Ellis said."

"I know!" said McGurk. "I'm only telling Officer Rockaway what The Voice told us. And since it's your walkie-talkies that have gotten us into this mess—"

"*I* can't help it if I stumbled into making a bunch of time machines, can I?" said Brains.

"You're really sure about that, aren't you?" I said. "I mean you really think these walkie-talkies—"

"Yes," said Brains. "It must have been something I did when I was modifying them. Some of the most important scientific discoveries were made by accident."

He was beginning to look proud.

"So long as they get us back to the twentieth century," said McGurk, "that's okay. *Then* you can brag."

"The Voice said this is the twelfth century," said Wanda.

"What did it say about this dragon?" I asked.

"It's killed more than a dozen knights already," said McGurk. "Knights who'd been going to the princess's rescue."

"Over a period of years," said Wanda. "And guess who wants to be next."

"I only said we'd investigate," said McGurk. "Dragon or not, if she's being held prisoner, that's unlawful imprisonment for starters. Felony one."

"Well, I guess we *could* take a closer look at the castle," I said.

"You bet, Officer Rockaway!" said McGurk. "It makes a lot more sense than standing around like dummies."

"Or statues," said Wanda, bending down and giving her legs a brisk rubbing.

"Right, men!" said McGurk. "So that's settled. Follow me."

We followed him. That's when we began to see what was on the other side of the hill: the stream at the bottom and the woods rising above it, halfway up the steeper hill to the castle, still gleaming white, still a few miles distant.

"If there *is* a dragon," said McGurk, as we scrambled down to the stream, "it'll—"

"Baloney!" said Brains.

"If there *is* a dragon," McGurk repeated, "it'll be lurking somewhere in the woods, closer to the castle."

"Oh, yeah?" murmured Wanda, suddenly looking scared. "How about down here, in the stream? Listen!"

From behind a clump of bushes at the edge of the stream, a most peculiar noise had started to come. Like the wail of bagpipes, only softer.

We instantly became statues again, this time of our own choosing.

"What is it?" whispered Willie.

"Who—who knows?" said Brains.

It was Mari who unfroze us.

"It is nothing dangerous," she said. "It is only a human voice, a young voice, singing an old plain song, a chant."

"You could have fooled *me!*" said Wanda, as the voice rose above the rippling of the stream, then sank again.

"Come on," said McGurk. "Let's take a look."

We followed him to the bushes. He parted a couple of branches. Then he grinned.

"A kid," he said. "About our age. Bathing his feet. Look. . . ."

Sure enough, there he was, a boy of about twelve,

with his back half turned to us. He was dressed in an old brown smock that looked like a converted burlap sack. On his head he wore a funny kind of dirty white cap, like a baby's bonnet or a nightcap, fastened under his chin.

But it wasn't his clothes that interested us most just then.

"Yik!" whispered Willie. "No wonder he's wailing and moaning! Look at those black snake things stuck to his legs."

Well, snakes, no. More like fat, black, garden slugs. Slowly curling and uncurling, swelling and throbbing.

Wanda was even more precise.

"They're not snakes," she said. "They're leeches. They suck human blood."

"No wonder he's trying to wash 'em off!" said McGurk, shuddering.

"He isn't trying to wash them off," said Wanda. "He's catching them, using his legs for bait."

"Huh?" McGurk was looking white.

"Yes," said Mari. "They used them—*use* them— for drawing blood from sick people. For healing."

"I copied a picture of a leech gatherer just like this," said Wanda. "For our class project."

She had, too. I remembered it now. Here is a copy of Wanda's picture, reproduced with her permission.

"Keep quiet, men!" whispered McGurk. "Don't let him see you. He might be the dragon's lookout. We'll cross the stream farther along. Uh—maybe there'll be some stepping stones."

The last bit gave away McGurk's real motives, I guess. The stream was shallow enough to wade through at any point. But he was more concerned about not getting leeches stuck to his legs, and I can't say I blamed him.

Even getting singed by a dragon's breath couldn't have been worse than having those fat, black, swollen worms sucking your lifeblood out through your ankles and calves.

We left the kid to his weird chanting, each of us thinking the same thing, I'm pretty sure.

Better him than us!

4 The Dragon

Well, farther along the stream there *were* some stepping-stones. So we crossed over on them and then took a path that went through the woods, twisting and turning but always climbing upward.

"Are you sure we're doing the right thing, McGurk?" I asked.

"This is all we *can* do," he grunted.

"But what if we meet the dragon?" said Willie.

"Baloney!" said Brains.

"We keep our eyes skinned," said McGurk, "and make sure we see it before it sees us. It's probably only on the lookout for men in shining armor on horses anyway."

Finally we got clear of the trees. We were much higher up, but the ground was so steep at that point that we couldn't see the castle.

"Where's it gone?" said Willie.

"What?" said McGurk.

"The castle."

Wanda turned from looking back at the trees, which had interested her greatly.

"Sometimes the nearer you get," she said, "the less you can see."

"Like you say about woods," said Mari. "Sometimes you cannot see them for the trees."

McGurk gave a cluck of impatience.

"Well, the castle's up here somewhere," he said. "There seems to be a dirt road over there. I bet you it'll lead us straight to it. Come on."

The road did in fact lead upward, but in a zigzag, taking the slope a little at a time. Above it, the bare ground wasn't as unbroken as it had seemed from a distance. It was full of folds and crevices.

In any one of which a dragon could be hiding.

Or a bunch of soldiers.

I frowned, feeling very uneasy all at once.

The road to the castle probably wasn't going to be such easy going as it had first looked.

And, sure enough, when we reached the first sharp bend, where the zig became a zag, we spotted it.

Or at least some of the others did.

"Gosh!" said Wanda, catching her breath.

"What?" I said, blinking.

"Up there along the road," said McGurk, grimly.

"The—the dragon!" gasped Brains.

"The creature that doesn't exist," murmured McGurk. "Never did. . . . Proceed with absolute caution, men. Be ready to yell and holler and make a lot of noise."

"Why, Chief McGurk?" asked Mari.

"To scare it," said McGurk. "It works with sharks and man-eating lions."

As we crept closer, I got a better look at it. Here's a drawing I made later, from memory:

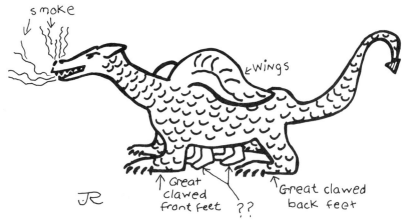

smoke

←Wings

↑ Great clawed front feet

?? ↑Great clawed back feet

JR

It looked very fierce with its smoking mouth and nostrils, its wings and its spear-tipped tail, its scaly body and its great clawed feet. But it wasn't making a lot of fuss. All it was doing really was blocking the road.

"It doesn't seem to have seen us yet," said Wanda.

"Maybe it's shortsighted," said Brains. "A lot of the early monsters were."

"Even those that never existed," murmured McGurk.

He wasn't shortsighted. His eyes were gleaming like a cat's as he paused, holding up his hand. The dragon was now only about one hundred feet away.

"There's something peculiar about this," said Willie, sniffing.

"Oh?" said McGurk, without taking his eyes off the beast.

"Yeah," said Willie. "It doesn't smell like a dragon."

"What *does* a dragon smell like, then?" asked Wanda.

"I don't know," said Willie. "But not like this. This smells like a moldy old cowhide rug we once had. Plus hot human bodies. Hot human bodies that haven't showered in months."

"Really?" I said, wondering if he was kidding.

But Willie rarely kids around. Especially when it comes to smells.

"Yeah," he said. "And make that hot human bodies that haven't showered in *years!*"

"Nice work, Officer Sandowsky," said McGurk. "And if you look close enough, you'll see their feet. It looks like there's two of them."

He was right. Those are the things I marked with a query in the picture. Even as McGurk spoke, those feet began to move and the dragon turned to face us. Those four *human* feet, I mean, not the great clawed ones. They just remained lifeless, hanging from the creature's body.

As well they might, of course, seeing they were only painted and stuck on.

"Anyone on horseback would never see those real feet," said McGurk. "But I did. . . . All right, you jerks!" he said, moving forward briskly now. "Come on out of there! The party's over!"

I gasped. He was taking a terrible risk. I mean okay, the dragon's body was just a fake, with a couple of people inside. But those two could have been real hoods, just as dangerous as any dragon.

They weren't, though.

As the body writhed and sagged and slowly crumpled to the ground, two kids stepped out. They, too, were dressed in coarse brown smocks, but they had nothing on their heads. Their hair looked as if it had once been golden, but now it was matted and dirty. And Willie was right. They did smell. Boy, did they ever!

"Please, go back! Go away!" said one of them. " 'Tis dangerous here!"

"Aye!" said the other. "Very dangerous. Especially for strangers."

The first one was a boy of about fourteen. He was still carrying carefully an iron pot with a handle and holes punched in its sides from which smoke was pouring out. I guessed there was burning rope in there. But even that didn't kill the basic stench of those kids.

"I'm Gareth," said the boy. "This is my sister, Gwyneth."

"We're twins," she said.

I could see that. They both had the same striking features: long upper lips over broad mouths. Even under the grease and the grime, you could tell that these were faces made for laughing.

But one look at their eyes, bulging slightly and terribly anxious, told me they hadn't laughed or even smiled in a long, long time.

And right now they looked scared. I suppose it was partly because we must have looked so strange to them in our outlandish gear. But partly it was also something permanent, some ongoing, never-ending terror.

"What were you doing in that dragon outfit?" McGurk asked sternly.

"We had had tidings that another knight was coming," said Gareth.

"Hoping to free the princess," said Gwyneth.

"But that is just an idle tale," said Gareth. "Melisande the Bad is nobody's prisoner."

"Who?"

"The princess," said Gwyneth. "Melisande the Bad."

"The dragon is just a decoy," said Gareth. He sounded sad now. "We have lured many a trusty knight to his doom."

"We and the ones before us," said Gwyneth. "The last two dragon-bearers got burned to death when the smoke bowl threw out sparks and the dragon cloth caught fire."

"So did the two before *them*," said Gareth.

"So why do you do it?" I asked.

"We have to," said Gareth. "We are her prisoners. We have to obey her every wish."

"Else we will be beheaded," said Gwyneth.

"Or worse!" groaned her brother.

McGurk turned. His eyes were glowing their greenest. His hair was shining its fieriest.

"Men," he said, "it looks to me like it's the dragon that wants delivering, not the damsel. The dragon's the one in distress!"

"Yes," began Gareth. "But—oh fie! Too late! Here comes Bluebeard—uh—Sir Boris the Bold and his men-at-arms! Now *you* will be taken prisoners!"

"Mother of Mercy!" moaned Gwyneth, trembling all over. "Oh, please do not tell them what we have said!"

There was no mistaking whom they had been referring to. The guy on horseback blocking our retreat down the road did have a beard that was black with a bluish tinge. His shield was painted the same dense black, but with a strong bright red wavy line slanting across it.

He wasn't looking very bold just then, however. Neither did any of the armed men who'd suddenly popped up from behind boulders and clumps of grass all around us. In spite of their swords and their daggers and maces and crossbows and the other weapons they were bristling with, they were keeping their distance, eying our strange clothes and black boxes like we might have been a bunch of aliens from outer space.

Which in a sense we were, of course.

"Take it easy, men," said McGurk. "I think we've got 'em fazed. Let's be sure to keep it that way!"

5 The Castle

While we were having this Mexican standoff with the princess's guards—with Sir Jack McGurk and Sir Boris the Bold, aka Bluebeard, staring each other down, green eyeball to black eyeball—this is a good chance to say something about the language problem.

Not that it was much of a problem. I mean, the twins and now Sir Boris and all the others we were to meet did speak English. And even though it was old-fashioned English, sometimes pronounced in strange ways, we very quickly got the drift of what they were saying. Being in a tight spot sure sharpens your wits—like when your life might depend on a single word. And even when the words themselves were different, the same thing applied. You could soon see what they meant by looking at the expressions of the speakers or where they were pointing.

Anyway, that's the spoken word. When they're written down they're much harder to follow. So in this record I'm cutting out most of the *thee*s and *thou*s and bringing it up-to-date so you'll read it the way we understood it when we heard it. I'll leave *some* of the old words in, just for the flavor. I've also included this copy of my list of old words for the class project, which could be useful:

Joey Rockaway

List of some of the words used in the age of Chivalry

thither = there   doth = do
yonder = there (espec. far away) hast = have
wist = know   quoth = said
Forsooth = in truth (sometimes used for sarcasm, like when we say "Oh, yeah?")
Eftsoons = soon after
Knave = a hood
caitiff = a jerk
villein = another jerk (also a peasant)
churl = a bad-tempered jerk.
Yclept or Clept = named
fowles = birds
a fool = a clown or jester (not necessarily an insult)
addle-pate = a dummy or dope
eln = the forearm

Now back to the fearful frozen moment.

McGurk spoke first, but only to us, in a low voice, still staring at Bluebeard.

"Men," he murmured, "switch your sets to receive. I'll leave mine on transmit. We might have to split up in a hurry."

Then, in a much louder voice, Bluebeard spoke to *his* crew.

"Take away their arms!" he snarled.

"But, sire," said one of them, "they do not have any."

"Seize those black purses, then!"

As some of the men moved nearer, five of those "black purses" suddenly crackled and sputtered and cried, "Hands off us, you dogs!"

The effect was dramatic.

Sir Boris's horse shied, nearly unseating him.

The men scattered backward, rolling their eyes and crossing themselves.

Even Gareth and Gwyneth clung to each other in obvious terror.

Boris the Bold recovered first. But he was one shook-up knight. His cheeks were very pale above the black beard and around his black glowing eyes.

"Forgive me, sir knight!" he said to McGurk (who was looking very pleased with himself at the effect his words had had). "What—what manner of magic is this? Purses that speak! From whence have you come?"

"From a great distance," said McGurk. He glanced up at the sky (on purpose, he told me later).

"And what do you mean by trying to steal our possessions? Are you a bunch of hoods, or what?"

"Hoods?" said Sir Boris.

"Footpads," I said. "A party of base footpads. Cutpurses and footpads!"

"Marry, no!" said Sir Boris, giving a great gulp that made his beard wag. "We are the personal guard of Her Highness the Princess Melisande. We—ah—we have come to escort you to the castle." (He was obviously making this up as he went along.) "We have come to escort you as her most welcome guests. And to see no harm befalls you. Come, let us go."

So, with the men-at-arms surrounding us—though still keeping their distance—and Sir Boris riding up behind and Gareth and Gwyneth bringing up the rear behind him, carrying the roughly folded up dragon outfit, our procession made its way up the road.

Nothing much happened on the way at first, so it gave us a good opportunity to look at some of the weapons these guys were bristling with. Willie was especially interested. His contribution to the class project had been a series of drawings of the arms of that period. He isn't a bad drawer and Ms. Ellis gave him an A, too. Here's his drawing of a sword just like the one Bluebeard was wearing, with his huge hairy right hand never far from the hilt:

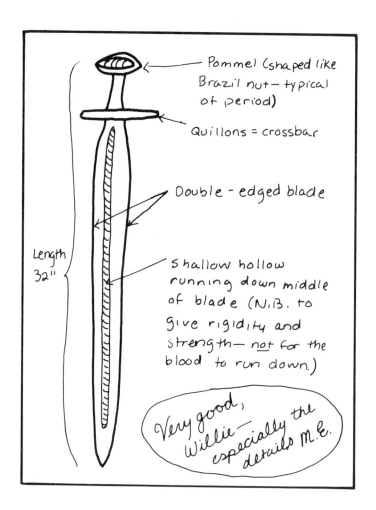

Pommel (shaped like Brazil nut— typical of period)

Quillons = crossbar

Double - edged blade

Length 32"

Shallow hollow running down middle of blade (N.B. to give rigidity and strength— not for the blood to run down.)

Very good, Willie— especially the details M.C.

"Thank goodness the sets seem to be working in daylight now," said Wanda, eying that sword.

"I guess it's because it's a different daylight," said Brains.

"Yeah—and a different *now*," McGurk murmured grimly.

As we got nearer to the castle, my heart began to sink. At the sides of the road at this point there were some solitary trees. They hadn't been notice-able from the hills where we'd first sighted the cas-tle. If we *had* been able to spot them from there, none of us would have taken a single step in that direction, I can tell you *that*!

Why?

Because hanging from those trees were the bodies of people—men, women, or children, it was hard to tell—all wearing those same rough burlap smocks.

"Rebels!" said Sir Boris, when Wanda gave a little scream and pointed at the first one we came to. "Thieves! Murderers! They deserved to die!"

We passed the others in stunned silence. A couple of crows flew up squawking from the last of them, the body of what looked like a four-year-old "thief" and "murderer." One of the birds flew straight to-ward our party. There was a swish as Bluebeard withdrew his sword and sliced it through the air in a flashing arc. The crow's body flopped to the ground, its wings still feebly beating. The head fell down among us, hitting Wanda on the back and leaving a smear of blood on her pink windbreaker.

"So perish *all* protesters!" said the bearded knight.

After that there was only one word for the castle,

as it loomed up in front of us on the last stretch of road.

Forbidding.

I mean, with that last ugly scene in our minds, it would have been all the same if it had been a five-star hotel we were being taken to.

But now, with its soaring towers and high walls, its drawbridge and its wide green-crusted stagnant moat, the castle looked awesome. The flag that fluttered from each of its towers seemed to match it, too: the same black and red design as on Bluebeard's shield. "As black as the heart of Princess Melisande," Gareth told us later. "With the wavy line as red as the stream of human blood she has been drinking for centuries."

Well, we didn't know about that just then. But that first impression of the castle gave us the same shuddery feeling. Under ordinary circumstances, the fact that the gleaming brightness of those walls as seen from a distance was really due to a coat or two of whitewash might have given them a familiar down-home look. But up close that whitewash was patchy, peeling in places, more gray than white, and it reminded me of the skin of some deadly poisonous toadstool.

"Pow!" gasped Willie, as we marched across the drawbridge over the murky water of the moat. He was clutching his nose and he looked like he meant to hold it that way for as long as we stayed at the castle. "That's nothing more than a—an open sewer!"

But McGurk was keeping his wits.

After we'd entered the courtyard and the big iron grill of the portcullis had slammed down over the entrance behind us—probably the only entrance and therefore only exit—he said, keeping his voice down: "Back on the road when they bushwhacked us, I didn't do such a bad imitation of the voice of the controller guy, did I?"

"No, Chief McGurk," said Mari. "It was very good."

"Thanks, Officer Yoshimura," he said. "Coming from you, that's real praise. But you're the expert. And next time we need his voice to scare them, I'll leave it to you. Okay?"

"Sure, Chief McGurk!"

I couldn't help admiring McGurk's quick thinking here. I mean it seemed like the controller, whoever he or it was, was only concerned in getting us located and wasn't going to intervene much to help us while we were here. This was going to be an ordeal, right enough—a real test of our resourcefulness.

"So switch *your* set ready to transmit," McGurk said to Mari. "The rest of us will keep ours switched to receive. Got that, men? Volume full up. I'll give you the nod when your input's required, Officer Yoshimura."

"Silence!" barked Sir Boris. We had gone through a gateway in an inner wall and come to a halt in front of a large studded door. He was beginning to look his true, bold, bullying self again. "Prepare to meet Her Royal Highness the Princess Melisande, whose word within her domain is Law, and whose Law is broken only upon the penalty of sure and certain Death!"

⑥ Princess Melisande

The studded door was in a part of the main tower that jutted out at the bottom, like a porch on an ordinary house. It was in fact itself much bigger than any ordinary house, but at the foot of that great soaring castle keep that's what it looked like. A mere porch.

Sir Boris left us waiting there, with the men-at-arms still standing guard behind us, while he went inside. During this wait I glanced around, trying to get our bearings.

So far, ever since crossing the drawbridge, I'd had an impression of thick walls, thick enough for men-at-arms to walk along the tops, behind the battlements. That much I'd expected. But what had surprised me was to see what was on the inside of those walls. It reminded me of all the dilapidated farms I'd ever seen, with lean-to shacks and sheds along the side of the walls, and geese wandering about and roosters and tethered goats and horses and at least one cow. There was also a battery of wooden cages containing chickens, all squawking and protesting as a dirty-looking girl plunged her hands in among them, swearing and squawking like an angry chicken herself as she collected their eggs. Like all the other people in those courtyards, she broke off when she saw us and gaped as we were escorted to the keep.

While we waited, one of the men-at-arms ordered the little knot of people that had drifted after us to get back to work.

"No, not you, Dickon, you dolt!" he said. "You have the right of entry at all times, as well you know!"

The boy who came pushing through, past us, was grinning. He was carrying a large bowl we'd seen before.

"Yik!" exclaimed Wanda, as she looked down at the mass of sluggish black bodies squirming inside. "It's the leech gatherer!"

Even Sir Boris treated him with gruff respect. He came out just at that moment and stood to one side to let the boy pass.

"Come on, lad!" he growled. "Don't take all day!"

Then it was our turn to enter, with Bluebeard leading the way and only two of the men to bring up the rear. All the rest, including the rubberneck-ers and Gareth and Gwyneth, had been left outside and told to get about their regular duties.

It was rather dim in there, even by contrast with

the gray daylight outside. But the smoky chamber we were led through was big enough for us to realize that this was the Great Hall Ms. Ellis had told us about. There were stacks of rough trestle tables and benches against one of the side walls. There was an open fire smoldering at one end, and at the other there was a low platform with a long table on it and high-backed chairs.

"It's just like the one that—" Mari began.

"Silence!" barked Sir Boris. He had paused in front of a doorway behind the platform. "Prepare to meet your hostess, the Princess Melisande. And take that bonnet off, you!"

He was pointing at my cap. I took it off and scrunched it in my hands. I was beginning to get very nervous again.

Then the bearded knight flung open the door.

And there, in that smaller inner chamber, we came face-to-face at last with the castle's evil owner.

Well, I have to admit that at first, anyway, she didn't *look* evil.

She was smiling, and there were dimples in her fresh, smooth, creamy cheeks. Her bright blue eyes were smiling, too, when she opened them wide with a flutter of dark lashes. The rest of her hair was a silvery gold that made even the small golden coronet she was wearing look dull. It was long hair and fell about her shoulders in waves that rippled whenever she moved.

Her gown was long, too, made out of some rich silken material, embroidered all over with red roses. She had to lift it from the floor with one hand all the time, and the sleeves were so wide that they drooped halfway to the floor. And what I'm getting at is this: She looked every inch a royal princess.

Standing on one side of her was another woman. She was taller and rather older. She wore a similar long-sleeved dress, but the material wasn't as rich. Also she had nothing on her head, and although her hair, too, was fair, it didn't shine like the princess's and instead of flowing in waves it hung down in two long plaited ropes at either side of her face.

I shuddered slightly. Whether it was those ropes of hair that reminded me of the ropes those poor people were hanging from outside, or whether it was her face, I don't know. I mean that *was* an evil face and it wouldn't have surprised me one bit to learn that *she* was Melisande the Bad.

It was thin and long and foxlike and deeply tanned. I learned later that this person, Lady Polly, the princess's lady-in-waiting, was nicknamed the Brown Vixen—and it fit. But just then I was wondering where I'd seen that face before. Also remembering Ms. Ellis saying it was very unusual for ladies in those days to have a tan, because it was considered ugly and too much like the peasant women who worked all day in the fields.

Sir Boris himself had gone to stand at the other side of the princess. And behind these three there hovered a man in a long black gown with a floppy black velvet cap. His hair was almost as long and bright as Princess Melisande's—but his was white. His face was very pale, too, but it was an amazingly young face for hair like that. Young but haggard, with dark sunken eyes that stared out at us suspiciously.

"This is my lady-in-waiting, Lady Polly," the princess said, with a slight gesture of the arm that set the wide sleeve rustling. "He who stands behind me is my chamberlain and adviser—my Lord Merlin Lestrange. And this one you know," she said, indicating Sir Boris.

Bluebeard bowed his head slightly, still glaring at us. And what with his glare and the chamberlain's stare and the lady-in-waiting's sly narrow glitter, I started to warm toward the princess. At least her wide blue eyes seemed friendly.

Then Lady Polly bent to Princess Melisande and whispered something while looking at McGurk. And when the princess's eyebrows went up in arches and she looked at McGurk, too, her eyes began to lose their friendliness and to gleam with something like greed, and I felt shivery again.

"So you are the leader?" she said. "The Knight

of the Flaming Hair?"

McGurk made a sweeping bow and said, "Yes, your highness. And of the Fiery Freckles. Some call me that."

I blinked. He was beginning to sound like a real knight.

"From whence have you come?" asked the princess.

"Many thousands of miles, ma'am, your highness. We—"

"And who are these with you?"

McGurk introduced most of us with our Age of Chivalry names: the Knight of the Seeing Nose, the Knight of the Questing Quill, the Artificer of Cunning Devices, and the Lady of the Woodlands. But when he came to Mari he dropped the Maid of Many Voices title and just called her Lady Mari, the Maid from the Orient.

I breathed a sigh of relief. It could have been disastrous to alert them to Mari's special talent when it looked as if our lives might depend on it before long.

Princess Melisande took the names in her stride. Only at Willie's did she seem slightly puzzled, and when McGurk had finished his introductions she asked him what this meant.

"His nose is so sensitive, your highness, it's like he can see with it," he replied.

She nodded and looked at Willie.

"Can you smell evil, sir knight?"

Willie looked confused.

"Uh—ma'am—"

"Can you sniff out treachery?"

"Well—" he began.

"Mayhap you might not be accustomed to treachery," she said. "But here I can find work for you, Sir Nose," she went on, just as if she were now talking directly to that organ and not its owner. "If your length speaks truly of your prowess."

There was no reply to that. Willie just gaped. Even McGurk had nothing to say.

Then she turned to him and smiled sweetly.

"Do you bring me gifts?"

McGurk still had nothing to say.

"Uh . . ."

"In those black purses," she went on, a little impatiently. "Do they contain gifts?"

Sir Boris bent to her, holding his beard so it wouldn't brush the royal shoulder.

"Your highness," he began, glancing uneasily at our black boxes, "they—"

"Do not interrupt, Sir Boris!" she snapped. "Collect them and bring them to me."

He took one slow uneasy step in our direction, then jumped and sprang back when five of those boxes began to speak in a voice of thunder coming through sizzling hail.

"Hands off those boxes! Touch nothing that is theirs! Disobey at your peril!"

If Sir Boris, who half expected it, jumped, you can imagine the effect on the others. The princess's coronet slipped sideways as she stepped back, her eyes wider than ever now, but with terror. The Brown Vixen fell to her knees. The chamberlain put up a trembling hand to shield his eyes.

The princess recovered first.

"Who—whose voice is that?" she whispered.

"Our controller," said McGurk, giving Mari a quick glance of congratulation. "The one who sent us here. Our guide. Uh—you know . . ." he ended lamely.

The answer seemed to satisfy the princess. Sir Boris nodded anxiously. The other two were still getting over it.

"How do I know you are not here to do me harm?" the princess asked.

"Because we aren't hoods, ma'am," said McGurk.

"Hoods?"

"I mean we are on the side of the law," he said. She frowned at this.

"On the side of the *king*?" she asked sharply.

"No, ma'am. We're private detectives. Look"—he fumbled in his back pocket—"here is my ID card."

This caused another little flutter. Without touching it, the princess stared at McGurk's photograph. She seemed awed as she glanced up at his face and then back to the picture.

"But this—this is so lifelike!" she said. She turned to me. "Did *you* paint this, Sir Scribe?"

I shook my head. I was thinking fast.

"No, your highness. Our photogr— our artist painted it."

She looked around at the others.

"Which one of you?"

"No, your highness," I said. "The artist didn't come with us. Uh—Sir Pola Royd stayed home."

She turned to McGurk and, with a stern regal look, said, "Then send for him!"

McGurk shook his head.

"It would take too long, ma'am."

"Fie!" Her blue eyes flashed. "You will be staying here as my guests until he comes and paints *my* portrait."

"He—"

"That is my wish. . . . What is that?"

She was staring at a crumpled dollar bill that had dropped out of the lining of my cap.

I pounced on it.

"What is that?" repeated Princess Melisande.

I had a sudden inspiration. I mean it was no use telling her what it really was. The only money she knew came in coins.

"Our passport, your highness," I said, as I picked it up.

She didn't know that, either.

"Your what?"

"Our—our warrant from our ruler," I said. "Asking that our movements may be kept free."

McGurk and the others were looking at me curiously.

"Show me!" said the princess. "Not too close," she added hastily, staring at what must have looked very strange to her.

Her three companions were looking just as cautious.

She touched the bill with the tip of one long fingernail.

"What is this substance?" she asked. "It looks too thin for parchment."

"Paper, ma'am," said McGurk, getting in on the act.

"That is correct, your highness," said her chamberlain. "Paper."

He pronounced it differently, more like they say it in French—*papiay*.

"Ah!" said the princess, her eyes lighting up. "I thought so. My cousin, Katherine the Callous of Catalonia, has been telling me about it. The Moors to the south, in Spain, have recently discovered it." She looked up. "Is *that* where you come from?"

"No," I said. "The U.S.A." She looked blank. I showed her the printed words on the bill:

She still looked blank. She obviously couldn't read it. In any case she seemed more interested in Washington's portrait. She pointed at it.

"Who is that?"

"The father of our country, your highness," I said.

"Your *king*?"

"Sort of."

She snapped her fingers.

"My lord chamberlain," she said. "What says this?"

He bent over the bill, his white face looking puzzled.

He couldn't read it, either.

"Has this scribe been lying to me?" she said, with an ugly glint in her eyes.

Then I remembered Ms. Ellis saying that even those who were literate at that time could only read and write in Latin. I turned the bill over.

"There," I said. "There's something you will understand."

I pointed to the picture of the front of the great seal.

The chamberlain bent over again.

Then suddenly stiffened.

"Y-yes, your highness," he said in a trembling voice. "Here indeed it does say something."

"Well—what?" she demanded.

He crossed himself.

"It says, your highness," he lowered his voice, " 'Annuit Coeptis—He has smiled on our undertakings.' And below that it says, 'Novus ordo seclorum—A new cycle of the ages.' "

"That's right," said McGurk, looking as smug as if he ever *did* know what it said. "A new world.

That's where we come from."

Everyone fell silent as the chamberlain bent to the great seal again.

"And there, see," he said in an awed voice. "A magic symbol. This edifice—this pyramid. With the eye."

"What does it mean?" asked the princess, looking a shade paler herself.

"He is one who is steeped in the wisdom of the pyramids—"

"The pyramids?" asked Lady Polly.

"Yes, my lady," said the chamberlain. "Spoken of by knights returning from the Crusade. A mighty potent symbol. And the eye is that of the One who sees everything."

"The father of our country, ma'am," said McGurk, looking eager. "Turn it over, Officer Rockaway." He pointed to our first president's face. "*He* is the one who sees everything. The one who sent us here. The one whose voice you have just heard."

"Aye, that is so!" boomed the voice of "George Washington" from five of our boxes, with Mari bending over hers as if to listen more intently. "I see all—*all*—and forget nothing!"

After that, we received only the greatest respect. The princess had been looking curiously at my and Brains's glasses, and I'd been expecting her to demand them from us and try them on. But not now.

"Lady Polly," she said, "conduct them to the large guest chamber. Allot them two servants and see that they are taken on a tour of the castle. And—" she added, eying my cap as I stuffed the green "warrant" back into its lining—"and see that they are given the freedom of the castle."

Sir Boris frowned.

"Even the dungeons, your highness?"

For a few seconds she looked very thoughtful. Then between those girlish dimples there appeared one of the thinnest, cruelest smiles I have ever seen.

"Why not?" she said. " 'Twill show them what happens to those who displease me!"

7 In the Dungeons

Lady Polly led the way along a passage just outside the Great Hall. It had more than Willie clutching the nose.

"The privy," said Lady Polly, with a wry smile, pointing to a door at the end.

Mercifully, she led us through another doorway and up a dark, narrow spiral staircase and onto a passage on the second floor.

"The large guest chamber," she said, opening the first door. "The *best* guest chamber."

She could have fooled me.

I mean it wasn't exactly the presidential suite. It was quite large, yes. But its ceiling was very low and its floor was covered with straw that didn't look any too clean. There were a couple of slits for windows—unglazed and drafty, of course. There was a big earthenware jug on a small table in one corner. In another corner there was a pile of narrow trundle beds. (Narrow? About one plank wide!)

"There are more than six beds there," she said. "So you have one each. Maybe two side-by-side for your leader. And there," she said, pointing, "are sufficient coverlets, I trow."

It looked like a stack of burlap sacks to me. In fact the cleanest, most luxurious cloth in there was hanging on one wall: an old faded tapestry depicting a party of knights in a woods with a castle showing through the trees.

" 'Tis rumored that King Arthur's queen, Guinevere, made that with her own hands," she said, when she saw me looking at it. "No!" she said to Willie, who was already picking out the top bed from the pile. "Leave that to your servants. I will be sending them in, shortly." Then she turned to McGurk. "And I *would* get them to show you the dungeons, if I were you. You will see one in there who will interest you mightily."

"Me?" said McGurk.

"Well," she said, "all of you. But you especially."

Then she left us while she went to drum up our servants.

"Well, at least," I said, "we get to keep our walkie-talkies."

"Yes," said McGurk, looking worried. "But not for long maybe. I mean they might begin to suspect they're bombs."

"Bombs!" exploded Brains. "Gunpowder hasn't been invented yet! Not in Europe."

"In China though," Mari began, "they—"

She broke off when Gareth and Gwyneth came into the room.

"We have been told to be your servants," said Gwyneth, looking rather excited and sounding out of breath.

"Yes," said Gareth. "And first we wish to thank you for not telling them what we told you."

"How do you know we didn't?" said McGurk.

"We still have our heads," said Gwyneth.

"We are not chained up in the dungeons with the others," said Gareth.

"What others?" said McGurk.

"Prisoners," said Gwyneth. "Knights like yourselves."

As the twins began to lay out the beds, McGurk questioned them.

"What is Princess Melisande *really* like?"

"A monster!" said Gareth.

"Some say she is hundreds of years old," said Gwyneth.

"She doesn't *look* it!" said Wanda.

"Of course not!" said Gwyneth. "That is why—" She broke off and looked nervously at her brother.

"Some say she is the sister of King Arthur," said Gareth. "Morgan Le Fay. A very wicked sorceress. And that Lord Merlin Lestrange is *the* Merlin. King Arthur's court wizard."

"But King Arthur lived in the fifth or sixth century," said Mari. "This is the twelfth."

"Which would make the princess more than six hundred years old," said McGurk.

"Yes," said Gwyneth, beginning to lay the pieces of sacking on the beds.

"But how does she stay so young-looking?" said Wanda.

"She drinks human blood," said Gwyneth, with a shudder.

"But only the blood of brave men," said Gareth.

"That is why she spreads this story about the dragon," said his sister. "Bluebeard and his men then capture them when they come thinking to rescue her."

"Her teeth looked all right to me," said Willie.

"Yes," said Gwyneth. "Her diet keeps them ever white and beautiful."

"No," said Willie. "I meant she doesn't have fangs. You know. Like Count Dracula."

"Count Dracula?" said both twins.

"A Rumanian," I said. "After your time. He had vampire's teeth to suck human blood from his victims' necks."

"Their carotid arteries," said Brains.

"Oh," said Gareth, "the princess does not suck it directly from *her* victims. She gets leeches to do the sucking and then she eats the leeches."

McGurk gulped noisily. He looked two shades

paler. We all fell silent.

Wanda spoke first.

"The leech gatherer," she said, with a shiver.

"That explains why even Sir Boris steps aside when he passes," said Brains.

"Yes," said Gareth. "Dickon is her most important servant. She makes sure he is always treated kindly. . . . But come," he said, "and we will show you around, as we have been charged to do."

"Uh"— McGurk cleared his throat—"she did say we could see the dungeons."

A scared look passed across Gareth's eyes.

"Well, if that is your pleasure," he said, "so be it. Pray, follow us."

We went down the stairs, this time continuing below the first floor: down, down, down, with only a faint red flickering from below to light the way.

Then we entered a kind of antechamber, with a couple of flaring torches on the walls, a table and two stools, on which were sitting two of the most villainous-looking men I have ever seen.

One was short and stocky, built like a barrel, with a hairy face and piggy little eyes. The other was tall and thin, with a wide, almost lipless mouth and glaring crossed eyes. The men seemed to have been taking turns drinking from the large jug on the table between them.

"Well?" grunted the short one, giving his companion the chance to snatch the jug and put it to that horrible slitty mouth. "What d'ye want?"

"The princess says we are to show these people the dungeons," said Gareth.

The tall man wiped his mouth with the back of a very dirty hand. He was grinning. It was like the grin of a corpse.

"And then to leave them here?" he said. "In chains?"

He nodded toward a dark recess in the opposite wall, where there was a long bench with chains hanging down over it.

"No, no!" said Gareth. "These are honored guests."

Both men stood up.

"Very well," said the fat one. "One moment."

He and his companion went to the wall, where we now saw that some black hoods were hanging, as well as the chains. They took the hoods down and put them on—and a terrible sight they looked, all in black, with their eyes glittering through the holes.

"What are these for?" said Gareth. "The hoods?"

"We wear them when we execute people," said the short one.

"But—but you are not going to do that now," said Gwyneth. "Are you?"

"No," said the tall one. Then he giggled and it was a sound that nearly froze my blood. "But we always put them on when we visit the prisoners. It frightens them famously."

The other man guffawed.

"They never know for sure if we are not come to hang them."

"Or behead them."

"Or to draw out their hearts and their lungs."

"Or their bowels and their puddings."

"But this is just our little jest," said the short one. "Really it is so that they will not recognize us, should they be ransomed and set free."

"One of them *is* the king's son, you know," said the other.

We followed them through what must have been the torture chamber, judging from the instruments I saw hanging from the walls, together with what looked like a selection of hanging ropes with varying sizes of nooses. Plus a large bloodstained table with straps and a wheel with a handle, and a helmet with hinges that gaped half open and showed the spikes that studded it *inside.* Not to mention a mess of smaller iron tools, like pincers and rings with screws in them and . . . It's no use. I break out in a sweat just thinking about them.

In any case, right then we were more interested in the noises coming from ahead.

Piteous groaning noises.

And then we saw them.

Those poor, weak, wasted shapes that shrank away from the bars of their cell as we approached.

And as they shrank away it reminded me of a couple of lines of a poem we'd had to learn for the class project. It was about a beautiful but merciless woman who snared knights into her clutches, just like Princess Melisande. Mari printed it in Old English lettering (she's almost as good at copying writing styles as she is at imitating voices). Here are those lines, taken from her copy:

> I saw pale kings and princes, too,
> Pale warriors, death-pale were they all

And here are another two lines that fitted perfectly what we were observing:

> I saw their starb'd lips in the gloam
> With horrid warning gaped wide

There were four of them, death-pale, starving and gaping, in that foul stinking cell.

"Which—which is the king's son?" Wanda asked, in a hushed voice.

"Prince Geoffrey?" said the fat man. "That one there," he said, dipping his torch in the direction of a bundle of rags and hair in a far corner. "Ho, your highness! Come and salute your visitors. Mayhap one has brought ransom enough to secure your release."

The bundle half rose. For a couple of seconds

eager eyes shone above the matted beard. Then they faded and he slumped back against the wall when the tall one jeered: "And mayhap *not!*"

"You dogs! You scum!" snarled another of the prisoners.

"Ah! The Irish princeling speaks!" said the tall man Then he giggled nervously and stepped back. Not only had this one spoken, he had also bounded forward and was shaking the bars.

We stared. Up front, in the light of the two torches, we could see him quite clearly. He had a flaming red beard, down to his waist. But that and his spirit were the only lively things about him. He was terribly thin. His green eyes had glowed momentarily, but they quickly dulled over, just as Prince Geoffrey's had done. He backed away slowly.

"If only your highness The McGurk would eat more food—" the fat man began.

"The *who?*" gasped McGurk—*our* McGurk.

"The McGurk," said the tall man. "He is an Irish chieftain."

"That is what they call them over there," said the other. "The McGurk, The O'Donovan, The This, The That."

"Instead of count or lord or duke," said his colleague.

"And he is the head of all McGurks?" said McGurk, his voice barely above a whisper.

"Yes," said the fat man. "His father died while this one was in here. So now *he* is The McGurk. We have had him since he was only thirteen. And a fine brave lad he was."

"Imagine," said the tall one—and he wasn't completely sneering—"imagine him coming to rescue a princess at his age."

"*I* can imagine it," murmured Wanda, glancing at our McGurk.

"That was seven long years ago," said the fat man.

I gaped. The poor guy looked more like eighty than twenty.

"But he has yielded to the princess many gallons of blood in that time," said the tall man.

"She still prefers his," said his companion. He smacked his lips behind the hood. "She says 'tis saltier and more flavorful than any other. As tasty as good beef stew.' "

"But, alas," said the tall one, "even though she sends him down the most toothsome dishes and dainties, he refuses to take more than bread and water."

"So that now," said the other, "even the thirstieth leech can draw from him no more than a thimbleful."

I suddenly began to realize what Lady Polly had meant about someone in there who would interest McGurk especially. Also why she had pointed him out to Princess Melisande when she first saw us.

With a long beard and the loss of twenty or thirty pounds he would have looked very like the Irish prisoner. And the Irish prisoner at his age, beardless and comparatively plump and juicy, must have looked very like *him*.

Right now, though, our leader was looking sick. Stunned and sick.

"Men," he murmured, as we went back up the steps for the rest of our tour, "we must rescue those prisoners."

"As well as *us*?" said Gareth, anxiously.

"As well as you," he said. "But especially The— The McGurk. I mean, he's got to be my great-great-great-grandfather."

"Great times twenty or thirty great-grandfathers," said Brains.

"Yeah," said McGurk, wearily. "And you know what? If he was taken prisoner when he was thirteen, the chances are he isn't married."

"So?" I said.

"So he won't have any kids," said McGurk.

"What does that have to do with anything?" said Wanda.

"And if he dies," McGurk went on, as if he hadn't heard her, "if he dies before he does get married and have kids—"

"Which looks likely," I said. "Unfortunately."

"Then he won't have any descendants," said

McGurk, with a terribly sad and haunted look in those green eyes. "Including *me!*"

We stared.

Now it was becoming clear. . . .

"So we just have to make sure he gets out of here alive, men," he said. "We just *have* to." He looked shocked and awed and terrified and determined all at the same time. "My—my future *existence* depends on it!"

8 The Special Dish

After a shock like that, it's no wonder we didn't take in many details on our tour around the castle. I mean, all right, we were shown the place where they kept the horses and the armory, the kitchen garden and the dairy (where everyone was bustling about, getting the ingredients ready for some kind of special banquet). But we weren't really interested. All the time that Gareth and Gwyneth were pointing these things out, we were on the lookout for escape routes. You know, things like holes in the wall, or doors that might lead to the world outside and didn't look particularly well guarded.

And how many of these possible escape routes did we spot?

Zilch.

Not one.

And what with the thickness of those outer walls and their height and the number of men patrolling the walkways on top of them, and the width of that moat, and the stoutness of the drawbridge (now up), and the obvious strength of the iron portcullis that backed it up—well, we became gloomier and gloomier.

"If we're going to rescue you," McGurk said to Gareth and Gwyneth at last, "you're going to have to help us get out of here."

The twins hadn't been looking any too happy either.

"Aye," said Gareth. "We have been thinking about that. And even if only one person had to escape, 'twould be difficult."

"Nigh impossible," said Gwyneth, sighing.

"But six of you and two of us—" Gareth shook his head.

"And—and even if we did all get out—privily, without being seen—where would we go?" said Gwyneth. "Sir Boris and his horsemen would soon chase us down when they discovered we had gone."

McGurk's freckles were clustering in a storm cloud.

"Well," he said, "don't give up hope. *We* never do. Right, men?"

Five doubtful grunting noises were all he got in answer.

"For instance," he said, giving us a quick collective scowl, "how about secret passages? *Aren't* there any in this place?"

Gareth and Gwyneth looked at each other, their faces wearing the same troubled frown.

"Well—" Gareth began. Then he broke off. We were standing next to a bed of herbs in the kitchen garden and Lady Polly was bearing down on us, her face looking foxier than ever.

"Ah, there you are!" she said. "I have been looking all over for you."

"Yes, ma'am?" said McGurk, trying to look bright and alert, as if he hadn't a care in the world.

"Yes," she said. She was smiling slyly. It was the kind of smile that said, You don't fool me for one minute, buster. But what she did say was, "Her highness sends her compliments and trusts you will be her honored guests at the banquet this evening."

"Banquet?" said Willie eagerly. He'd already been complaining of how empty he was feeling.

"Yes," said Lady Polly. "So be sure to bring your appetites. Princess Melisande hates those who come to her table without. She has been known to have pickers and peckers and pushers-away-of-plates— miserable sparrows, she calls them—cast into the dungeons. And you two"—she turned to the twins— "you will be helping to serve, so get you to the kitchen now."

Well, the bit about being cast into the dungeons didn't do much for our appetites. Even Willie started to look like he was no longer in the mood for eating. But we needn't have worried. By the time someone sounded a great gong to summon us to the banquet we'd been made ravenous by the delicious smells that started seeping and curling and wafting around the passages and chambers of the keep.

I mean—well—here are just a few of the items on the menu:

Freshly caught fish, broiled and stuffed with roasted almonds

Tender young suckling pig, roasted whole and served with apples and quinces

Roast pheasants

Plum pie with clotted cream

Apple pie, the same

Hot pancakes stuffed with honey

Those were some of the dishes for the princess's table, on the platform. It had been covered with white cloths and decked out with silver cups and plates and spoons. (Except that at the bottom end of the table, where we were placed, the cups were made of wood, with only the rims silver.)

The people at the trestle tables in the body of the hall had to make do with earthenware cups and wooden plates and spoons. But even they didn't fare so badly. Here's a quick selection from *their* menu.

Thick rich soup, with dumplings

Chicken stew

Eel pie

Pancakes with honey

Now all right. I wouldn't have touched that eel pie (which was on our menu as well) with a forty-foot spoon, once I'd been told what was in it. But it did smell good. And there were other pleasantly smelling things, too, that I wasn't keen about, on our table. Like a pig's head brought in steaming on a plate, with its cheeks served in slices. And a pie that someone said was filled with broiled skylarks and was supposed to be a great delicacy. Thankfully, we didn't have to eat something of everything. So long as you ate heartily what you *did* choose, you were safe.

As for drinking, there was wine for those at the princess's table and jugs of beer or cider for the others. Right at the start, we were offered wine, but McGurk frowned at us and said, "Not while we're on duty, men." So we were given goat's milk instead, which some of the others seemed to like, especially Mari, who got herself a little white mustache with drinking it so eagerly. But me—no, sir! I just wet my lips with it, pretending to drink and hoping this wouldn't get me classed as a sparrow.

Nobody seemed to notice, however, even though we did come in for a lot of attention at first, mainly from the people at the lower tables—men-at-arms and other members of the castle staff. They kept looking at us and making comments to each other for the first ten minutes or so. But since most of them had already seen us before, either when we were first brought in or during our tour of the castle, they didn't keep it up. They soon became more interested in their food, and that went for those at the top table, too. I tell you: I've never seen so many people gobbling their food so eagerly, even at the school Christmas party. Some of the big hunting dogs who were sitting by their masters waiting for tidbits seemed dainty eaters by comparison.

As for the seating arrangement at the top table, here's a rough plan of it:

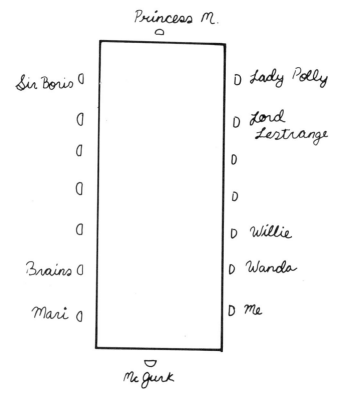

Those just shown by dots were other knights and ladies, whose names I didn't catch. And the reason I'm going into such details about the seating arrangements is this: Lady Polly had already explained to us that as honored guests we'd normally have been placed near the princess, but as kids we'd been put at the lower end.

Well, we soon guessed that that wasn't the whole truth, and that really it was because the princess was very uneasy about us overhearing some of the things she was saying. I mean, every so often I'd see her murmuring something to Sir Boris or Lady Polly or one of the others, with them looking at us as she spoke and either nodding or shaking their heads.

"I'd give anything to know what they're talking about," said McGurk, anxiously. "You don't happen to read lips as well as throw your voice, do you, Officer Yoshimura?"

"Sorry, Chief McGurk," said Mari, lifting her nose out of her cup of goat's milk and sighing. "No."

The first dish to be served at the top table was the fish stuffed with almonds, and it was good. Even before he'd eaten a mouthful, Willie said it was the best thing that had happened to his nose since we'd hit the twelfth century. At the other tables, they were starting with the thick soup and dumplings.

Soon everyone was biting and chewing and swallowing away, and talking and laughing, including us—except we didn't do much laughing—and the general noise level became quite high.

But then, suddenly, toward the end of this course, there was a hush, so that Willie was caught out and everyone heard him say, "Boy, but this fish is *good!*"

Nobody laughed. Some even frowned. Then we realized that the silence had been caused by Dickon. He had emerged from the door leading to the spiral staircase and was now slowly approaching the top table with a silver dish—a deep dish with a high domed lid. The tip of his tongue was sticking out with concentration and his eyes were crossed as they focused down on the dish. A man-at-arms at a lower table reached out and held his dog firmly by the scruff of its bristling neck to make sure Dickon didn't stumble over it. The dog must have been some kind of bloodhound. It certainly seemed very interested in that dish as it strained forward, growling and slavering.

Finally the boy reached the high table, placed the dish in front of Princess Melisande, bowed, then lifted the lid for her to inspect the contents.

Frowning slightly, she nodded. Then she picked up her spoon and got busy.

"Oh, no!" whispered Wanda. "Chopped leeches!"
She was right.

And what made it an even uglier spectacle was the fact that the leeches were in four sections inside the dish, each separated from the rest by a hedge of watercress or some other green garnishing. Nor was this all. Each section had a wooden toothpick stuck into it, with a little parchment flag at the top. According to Gareth and Gwyneth, who explained it to us later, each flag displayed the colors of the knight those leeches had been sucking: a red and gold one for Prince Geoffrey, a green one for The McGurk, and so on.

It took Princess Melisande less than three minutes to empty that bowl, she ate so greedily. But when she had finished and pushed it away, she looked more relaxed. Smiling around, all pink and dimpled, she nodded again and ordered some minstrels at the back to play lutes, bagpipes, and a harp.

Then a kind of collective sigh went around the hall and they all began eating and drinking noisily again.

Princess Melisande was a lot easier after that.

While we were tackling the crispy brown roast pheasants, one between two of us, and the people at the lower tables were getting stuck into their eel pies (which I wouldn't have touched with an *eighty*-foot spoon after seeing the princess eat those leeches)—while this was going on, Princess Melisande kept sending down silver plates with special tidbits "just for you, Sir Jack."

At first, McGurk tended to preen himself at this honor. Then Wanda reminded him that there was someone else, down below, whom the princess used to send dainties to, and all at once he lost his appetite.

"You don't really think she's got ideas about *my* blood, do you, Officer Rockaway?" he murmured.

"Well, you never know," I whispered. "That woman is a—a she-devil!"

"Sir Scribe!"

I jumped. I *felt* my face go white. For a second there I thought *she* must have been able to read lips.

"Y-your highness?" I stammered.

"Pray, why do you wear those crystal things on your nose?"

I guessed she meant my glasses.

"To see better, your highness," I said, feeling vastly relieved.

"May I try them?"

"Of course, your highness."

I took her the glasses. She inspected them for a moment, then put them on.

And screamed.

"Everything is blurred!" she cried. "He has bewitched me!"

Sir Boris sprang to his feet, hand on dagger. "By the—"

But the princess had taken them off and was laughing.

"I can see again!" She turned to me. "If you can see better with them, Sir Scribe, you must indeed be blind without them. Here"—she handed them back—"put them on again before you stumble onto the point of Sir Boris's dagger."

A chair scraped back at the other end. It was Brains, always anxious to get in on the act.

"Mine are even stronger, your highness!"

But Princess Melisande no longer wished to know and Brains was left to try to explain about contact lenses to the lady at his side, which only caused disbelieving laughter all around, much to his indignation.

Then the princess created another diversion.

"Pray, child," she called out to Wanda, "what is that magic golden ribbon with which you open and close your doublet?"

Wanda, who must have been feeling too warm,

had just unzippered her windbreaker.

"This, your highness?" she said, zippering it up again.

Some of them gasped. Princess Melisande nodded.

"Yes."

"It's a zipper, your highness."

"We all have them, your highness, on our—"

"Sit down, Officer Bellingham!" growled McGurk.

He, like me, mustn't have fancied the idea of giving them a demonstration with the zippers on our jeans.

"Come hither, child," said the princess to Wanda.

Very gingerly, she put out a hand to Wanda's windbreaker and began zippering up and down.

" 'Tis truly magic!" gasped Lady Polly.

"Yes," said the princess. "Or a very cunning piece of metalwork." She turned to Sir Boris. "Have Piers the armorer brought to me. Now."

Piers, who had been peacefully eating eel pie and minding his own business at one of the lower tables, was a thin, grizzled, wizened little guy.

"I wish you to make me twenty of these, Master Armorer," said the princess, zippering up and down again.

The armorer's eyes were small and sunken in a

mass of wrinkles, but for a moment they seemed to pop out as he peered at the zipper.

Then he sucked air in noisily through his teeth as he shook his head.

"I will try, your highness, but—"

"No buts!" she snapped. "You will do it!"

Piers sighed. "I will examine it more carefully in the morning, your highness. When the light is better."

"Just as you please, Master Armorer. So long as you make me twenty like this within one month."

A much soberer and sadder armorer went back to his table.

"One month!" Princess Melisande sang out after him. "Or you forfeit your head!"

There was a roar of laughter from farther up our table.

The princess scowled.

"Who dares laugh at me?"

Sir Boris got to his feet again and bowed low.

"No, your highness. We were not laughing at *you*. It was this one." He pointed at Brains and sat down. "He says—he says in his country—there are"— he could hardly get on for laughing again—"there are machines that take men up into and above the clouds, and—hoo! hoo!—travel faster than arrows, your highness—while—while"— he was thumping the table as he doubled up with laughter—"while the people inside are served—served with banquets like this!"

"But it's true!" bleated Brains. "Some of the machines carry five or six hundred people!"

Now the princess herself was laughing. She turned to Lady Polly and, still giggling, said something in her ear.

Lady Polly was grinning as she left the table and went into the room at the back. She wasn't long before she returned and placed something that jingled on the table.

Princess Melisande stood up and beckoned to Brains. When he reached her she handed him the object, holding it up as she did. It was a cap and bells, like the one the joker in a pack of playing cards wears.

"I hereby appoint you court jester," she said.

Brains looked flabbergasted.

"But—but don't you have one already, your highness?"

"He died last week," said the princess.

"What of?" asked Brains, looking down at the jingling headgear doubtfully.

"Oh, nothing catching," she said. "He died of bad jests. He told one too many. And now he has no head to put these on."

"But—but—" Brains was blinking helplessly.

"Well," said Princess Melisande, "don them your-self. Then jest on, good Fool!"

So poor Brains put on the cap and bells, took a deep breath, and started to tell them the one about carts that went without horses, carts that could go ten times faster than the swiftest horse.

Which had them all falling about with laughter and him protesting that he was simply telling the truth, which only had them laughing louder than ever.

Them, of course. Not us.

"The dummy!" groaned McGurk. "She'll *never* let us leave now!"

9 The Secret of the Tapestry

"We've got to get out of here!" said McGurk, when we were back in our chamber.

"You bet!" croaked Brains, hoarse after his one-man comic show. He flung down his cap and bells. They jingled mockingly before landing on his bed.

"Out of *here*? This room?" said Willie.

"No," said McGurk. The flickering light from the torch in its rack on the wall seemed to be making his freckles dance. But it was a slow, dismal funeral dance. "Out of this castle. And take Gareth and Gwyneth with us—so quit looking so worried, you two."

The twins were siting on the edge of one of the beds.

"Thank you," murmured Gareth. "But 'tis easier said than done."

"Yes," said Gwyneth, sighing. "You are allowed to move freely within the castle walls but . . ."

She broke off, sighing again.

"I mean all right," said McGurk, gloomily. "We're welcome guests so far. And we still have them fazed with our black boxes. But—well . . ."

"Well what?" said Wanda.

"Well, sooner or later, Officer Bellingham is going to run out of scientific marvels to make them laugh at, and then . . ."

He trailed off again.

"Then—what?" whispered Brains.

"You know very well what," said McGurk.

"Yeah," grunted Brains, his shoulders suddenly slumping.

"Please don't look so sad, Brains," said Mari. "There are hundreds of inventions and discoveries to tell them about. You could go on as long as the lady in the Arabian Nights did."

"Yeah," growled McGurk. "But before that, The McGurk down below might die or—or just dry up."

I nodded.

"And she's going to get very impatient when Sir Pola Royd doesn't show," I said.

"Not to mention when poor Piers fails to make her twenty zippers," said Wanda.

"Which he will," muttered Brains. "However clever he is, he just doesn't have the necessary technology."

"So then," faltered Wanda, "then she'll get the idea of killing us and—and taking over *our* zippers."

McGurk clapped his hands.

"Okay, men, that's enough of the negative. Let's concentrate on the positive." He turned to the twins. "Couldn't we just say we feel like going out for a stroll on the hillside?"

"The guards would stop you at the gates," said Gwyneth. "Even if the drawbridge *is* down."

"Yes, but—" McGurk began.

"There is a special security warning," said Gareth. "It is rumored that King Henry and a hunting party is in the forest only three leagues hence."

"Three miles?" said Willie. "That isn't far—"

"He said three *leagues*," rasped Brains. "That's more like nine miles."

"A long walk even if we did get out," said Wanda.

"Hey!" said McGurk, turning to the twins. "If he's that close, why doesn't he come and free his son?"

"He does not know Prince Geoffrey is here," said Gareth. "She has not asked a ransom for him. She is more interested in having the royal blood to sup on."

"While it lasts," said Gwyneth. "Poor Prince Geoffrey is very weak."

The gloomy cloud settled around McGurk's eyes again.

"Yeah—so are they all. All four of them." Then he brightened a little. "By the way—what about that secret passage you were going to tell us about?"

"Well, it is very doubtful," said Gareth. "But if it exists at all, now—*if*—it comes out—"

He got to his feet and looked at the tapestry on the wall. In the flickering torchlight, those old faded figures of the knights in the forest glade seemed to be moving.

"It comes out *here*," said Gareth.

He was pointing to the hillside just below the castle that could be seen through the gap in the trees.

"Behind the tapestry?" asked Wanda.

"No. *In* the tapestry," said Gareth. "If you look closely you will see that it is *this* castle that is depicted."

We all stared up at it.

"Yeah," said McGurk. "So it is. So?"

"So here," said Gareth, "just below, this rosy bower—dost see it?"

We moved closer still. Sure enough, there was a kind of cave entrance there, with roses all around it, badly faded but still visible. And also—I pushed my glasses farther down my nose—yes—

"A woman," I said. "Knitting or something."

"Yes," said Gwyneth. " 'Tis said to be the queen or princess who lived here once, hundreds of years ago, working on this very tapestry."

"She used to steal out of the castle to meet her lover there," said Gareth. "Some say it was Queen Guinevere herself and that this one"—he tapped the picture where one of the knights was looking over his shoulder, up at the castle—"this is Sir Lancelot, her lover."

"But she was *married*!" said Brains, looking horrified. "To King *Arthur!*"

"So what?" said Wanda, with a small smile. "She was having an affair with Sir Lancelot, wasn't she?"

"Quiet, men!" snapped McGurk. "We are *not* a bunch of divorce detectives." He turned back to Gareth. There was an eager gleam in McGurk's eyes now. "So what you're saying is she used a secret passage out of the castle to get to this rose place?"

"Verily," said Gareth. "But 'twas so long ago—"

"So *where* in the castle?" said McGurk. "Where's the other end, *this* end?"

Gareth and Gwyneth looked at each other uneasily.

"Where?" insisted McGurk.

Gareth sighed.

"Alas, the dungeons."

"Right under the noses of the jailers," said Gwyneth. She shuddered. "Carl and Wilfred. Whom you have met."

"Aye," said Gareth. "The Terrible Twain. Who live and eat and sleep down there, they so love their work."

I sighed, myself.

"So that rules that out," I said.

"Aye," said Gareth. "But 'tis only an old tale. And even if it did once exist, 'tis probably filled in by now."

"Oh, if only we had a barrel of gunpowder!" groaned Gwyneth.

Gareth gave her a sharp look.

"But we don't, so that is that," he said. "But mayhap there is another way."

"What?" said McGurk, eager again.

"When they let us out, Gwyneth and I, for dragon practice tomorrow . . ."

"Oh?" said McGurk. "Go on!"

Gareth shook his head.

"I must give it more thought," he said. "I will let you know first thing in the morning."

But McGurk was already ahead of him.

"You mean you might be able to *smuggle* us out?" he said. "Under the dragon outfit?"

"Aye," said Gareth, cautiously. "We *might*. But 'tis by no means certain. . . . Come, Gwyneth. Let us get some sleep. If it is to work at all we shall need to be fresh and alert."

"Yes, men," said McGurk, now looking brighter than he had all evening. "Let *us* try to get some shut-eye, too."

After Gareth and Gwyneth had gone to their quarters, we lay on our beds and watched the flickering shadows become slower and deeper, not saying anything but hoping a whole lot. Then I began to doze off and dream that Queen Guinevere had risen from her seat in the rosy bower and was now beckoning to me.

"Have faith, Sir Scribe," she said, in a low fluting voice. "All is not lost. And tell Sir Jack Lancelot—"

What she wanted me to tell him I'll never know, because at that moment Sir Jack or Sir Lancelot or whatever she liked to call him suddenly sat up in the bed next to mine and said, *"Hey!"*

Some of the others were so startled that they jumped out of *their* beds.

"What?" I said.

"Gwyneth!" he said.

"What about her?" said Wanda.

"What she *said*!" said McGurk. "Something about wishing we had a barrel of gunpowder!"

"Well, so do I," said Wanda. "But we don't have. So—"

"Don't you see what I'm getting at?" said Mc-Gurk. "Gunpowder hasn't been invented yet!"

"In China—" Mari began.

"In China, sure!" said McGurk. "But this isn't China. It wasn't discovered in Europe until—uh—"

"Gosh, yes!" said Wanda. "The fourteenth century. Ms. Ellis told us. And this is still the *twelfth*!"

"Maybe she meant something else," I said.

"Yeah!" grunted McGurk. "But in the morning I aim to find out!"

10 The Trojan Dragon

But in the morning McGurk didn't get to question Gwyneth about the gunpowder. He was much too preoccupied. So were we all.

Gareth wakened us very early, just before dawn.

"We must leave soon, while the light is still dim and before the guards are relieved," he said. "Those on duty now will be sleepy and less alert."

He led us down into the courtyard. There, in a shadowy corner, was Gwyneth with the dragon skin. Dawn was just beginning to break. One of those cold gray ones.

"It'll be a tight fit," said McGurk, frowning at the crumpled scaly body.

"All the more reason to leave in poor light," said Gareth. "Quick, get in. The tallest at the front with me, the smallest in the rear with Gwyneth."

Well, here is a sketch plan of that dragon, with us inside.

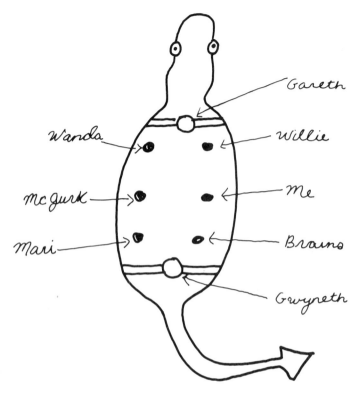

Gareth and Gwyneth took the weight of the dragon on their shoulders, using the wooden crossbars at the front and rear. We others had nothing like that to do. But, boy, McGurk was right! It was a *very* tight fit in there. The diagram doesn't show that, of course, with us only being represented by dots.

" 'Tis a good thing we don't have to use the smoke bowl on practice," said Gwyneth.

"You can say that again!" muttered Willie. "The smell of this old cowhide is bad enough!"

"Try to keep in step," said Gareth. "You taller ones bend at the knees."

"Why?" said Wanda.

"So the dragon skin isn't hoisted high enough to show too many feet and legs," said Gareth.

We bent our knees.

"Good!" said Gareth. "Now we will go to the drawbridge and hope for success."

We shuffled off—awkwardly at first, but soon in some sort of regular step. I couldn't help thinking of how it was like the Trojan horse. You know. The big wooden one that all those Greek soldiers got into to smuggle themselves inside the walled city of Troy. Only we aimed to get *outside* these walls, of course. And this was a ratty old cowhide dragon, not a wooden horse. A Trojan dragon . . .

It seemed to take forever, but really it was only a minute or two before we reached the main gate.

"Stop! Who goes there?" said a sleepy voice.

"Dragon," said Gareth.

"With whom inside?" asked the guard. This might have caused us some alarm, but he said it in a mechanical way, as if it were all part of a familiar routine.

"Gareth and Gwyneth Owen," said Gareth. "As usual."

"What is thy business, Dra-drag-ooon?" said the guard, finishing on a yawn.

"Dragon practice," said Gareth. "To practice our roaring and squirming and the lashing of our tail in the open countryside."

"Why there?" asked the guard.

I guessed this wasn't a part of the regular line of questions, because Gareth seemed to have to think how to answer.

Then he said, "So we will not awaken any soul in the castle. With our roaring."

"And will not knock anything over with our tail," said Gwyneth.

"Huh—" grunted the guard, sounding now as if *he* had to think. "Huh—by—uh—"

"By whose orders?" said the voice of another guard, prompting him.

"Yes! By whose orders?" said the first guard.

"By the orders of Her Highness the Princess Melisande," said Gareth.

"Who was up late last night and does not wish to be wakened early," said Gwyneth.

"Uh—well—one moment, Sir Dragon." The guard's voice then changed direction. "Lower the drawbridge!" he called out.

We all breathed a sigh of relief.

Then there was a clanking and churning and creaking.

"The drawbridge," whispered Gareth. "One more

minute and we will be outside."

We waited in dead silence, with our knees bent and our leg muscles aching terribly.

There was a final heavy thud.

"Very well," came the first guard's voice. "Pass, Dragon, and go about thy business."

We began to move forward. And this time— whether it was because of the cramp in our muscles, or our eagerness to be on our way, I don't know— but we started to shuffle away clumsily. So clumsily that Brains trod on my heel and—

"Oh, no!" I gasped, as I felt my left shoe slip off.

But the others were all moving forward by now, so there was nothing else for it but to leave it behind.

Then: "Ho!" came the shout.

And: "Dragon—hold!"

Well, we hadn't even reached the boards of the drawbridge by then. The paving stones were still hard and cold under my shoeless left foot.

So we halted and bent our knees again.

"Come out from under there!" said one of the guards.

"Leave this to me," whispered Gareth. "When I step out, all of you sink down except Gwyneth." Then, raising his voice, he said, "Here I am, guard. What is amiss?"

We sank down as he'd said, hoping it looked like

there was only Gwyneth left.

"No, not you!" we heard the guard say. "The others."

"I think he means me," said Gwyneth. "Sink down lower."

And she stepped out, too, leaving us all in a crumpled heap under the dragon outfit.

"Not you, either!" said the man, lifting the edge of the dragon skin and letting in daylight. "The owner of *this!*"

Well, *"this"* of course was this:

The left foot of my almost new size six Nike running shoes, complete with Velcro straps and looking not at all medieval. That is why I've drawn it with a jagged border—to show the shock that its sudden appearance must have given the guard. (And some of the would-be escapers, too, when they saw it in his hand and realized what had happened.)

In fact those shoes had been the target and envy of many eyes over the last twenty hours or so, and there was really no mistaking whom they belonged to.

"He's just been playing with us!" muttered McGurk, crawling out from under.

Already someone was ringing a loud bell and the drawbridge was on its creaking way up again.

But the worst sound was the clatter and patter of many feet, and before we knew it we were surrounded by men-at-arms, some of them only half dressed.

Sir Boris himself was cursing and pushing his way through them. He was still in his nightshirt, with his beard in a kind of hair net. I guess it would have looked funny if it hadn't been for the sword in his hairy hand.

"So!" he growled, glaring at McGurk.

Lord Lestrange was right behind him. He was in his usual black robe, with the puffy black velvet cap on his head, like he either slept in them or never went to sleep at all.

There was a sneer on his bloodless lips. There usually had been when he'd looked at us, but this time his eyes were bold and triumphant, not uncertain and shifty.

"Seize those boxes!" he said, quietly but firmly.

Only three or four of them had been switched to receive—we'd been so taken by surprise. But Mari did her best.

"Take not anything that is theirs!" those boxes boomed.

Once again, Sir Boris and his men recoiled, looking scared.

But Lord Merlin Lestrange only smiled.

"Pray, do as the Wizard Washington requests," he said silkily.

"But—" gasped Sir Boris.

"Leave them their clothes and their shoes and the crystal things on the noses of those two," said Lord Lestrange, still smiling his cold nasty smile. "But take away the boxes."

"But you just heard what—" began Bluebeard.

"The Wizard Washington says take not anything that is *theirs*," said Lord Lestrange. "But the boxes cannot be theirs because obviously they are *his*. And he said naught about not taking anything of *his*. Here!" he said, suddenly moving forward. "I will do it myself, under the protection of my own magic!"

Before Mari could work out exactly what he had meant, Princess Melisande's chamberlain had snatched off our walkie-talkies and placed them in a sad silent bundle on the ground.

This gave Sir Boris and the others courage.

"Right!" said the bearded knight. "We will take

these villains before her highness now!"

So, prodded by swords and the business ends of pikes, we were herded into the chamber at the back of the hall again.

We had to wait about ten agonizing minutes before Princess Melisande emerged from behind a room-dividing curtain, fully dressed and immaculately made-up. But this time she was furious.

And she, too, must have taken heart at the silence of those black boxes, which Lord Lestrange had placed carefully on a small table, after making some magic passes over them.

"You are nothing but spies and traitors!" she said, her eyes flashing blue lightning. "*You* six have been sent here by my enemies, no doubt with the knowledge of the king himself. And *you* two are their treacherous aiders and abetters! Am I not right?"

None of us said a word. What *was* there to say?

"Speak when the princess commands it!" barked Sir Boris.

"We have the right to remain silent," mumbled McGurk.

"So!" hissed Princess Melisande the Bad, living every inch up to her nickname now. "You will be slowly tortured until your tongues are loosened! Then they will be cut out!"

Lady Polly bent and whispered something in her ear. She only scowled the more fiercely.

"I care not about their blood or their jesting or their magic ribbons now!" she snarled. "Nor about Sir Pola Royd, who is obviously another plotter and will be put to death the moment he arrives. I cannot afford to have such dangerous back-stabbers under my roof for a single day." She turned to Sir Boris. "Take them to be tortured!" she spat.

"May I remind your highness that today is the sabbath?" said Lord Lestrange, looking slightly worried.

There must have been some very powerful belief about that. Mad as she was, Princess Melisande bit her lip and said, "Ah! Yes. Very well. Let the torture commence one minute after midnight. Meanwhile, take them out of my sight! To the dungeons with them!"

11 Other Time Travelers?

So that's how we came to end up in the castle dungeons. On the bench in the dark recess in the jailers' anteroom. With our hands and feet locked in the chains that hung from the wall. I guess we must have looked like a bunch of frightened marionettes waiting for the final scene in a gruesome puppet play.

As for the black boxes, they'd been taken prisoner, too. Lord Lestrange had advised that they should be executed along with us, as if they had lives of their own.

"Though handle them with great caution!" he had warned the jailers.

So now the walkie-talkies lay in a silent heap inside a wire cage that looked like a rat trap, just a few feet in front of us, next to the jug on the jailers' table.

They were in high glee, I can tell you: Carl and Wilfred, aka the Terrible Twain! They'd already put on their hoods.

"Oh, what sport we will have after midnight!" gloated Wilfred, the tall one.

"Aye!" said the short barrel one, Carl. "What pincing and piercing!"

"What stretching and squeezing!" said Wilfred.

"What crushing and crunching!" said Carl.

"And what songs we shall get them to sing!" said Wilfred.

"What screaming and sobbing!" said Carl.

"And what dancing they will do!" said Wilfred. "What writhing and wriggling!"

"What twitching and twisting!" said Carl. "But, hey—Wilfred—all in one spot. Never moving so much as an ell out of range of *our* musical instruments!"

"And what—" began Wilfred.

He broke off as Dickon appeared with a wooden tray on which there were four large steaming bowls. He placed it on the table.

"Prisoners' breakfasts," he announced. "The four regulars, mind . . . Not *them*," he added, glancing at us with a foolish grin.

Carl gave him a light cuff on the ear.

"Do not try to tell us our job, lad," he said. "We have had our instructions from your betters."

Dickon shrugged as he looked at us.

"She was going to have that one fattened up with fine meats and choice viands," he said, nodding toward McGurk. "And then he was to be drained by the thirstieth leeches I could gather."

"But not now," said Wilfred. "Not after being caught dealing treacherously. The princess will never drink the blood of base traitors."

"Now get back to thy regular leech-gathering, lad," said Carl. "While we feed what will be the *leeches'* breakfasts."

" 'Tis the sabbath," said Dickon. "No leech-gathering till the morrow."

"Good!" said Carl. "Then do not disturb us for the rest of this day. We have many preparations to make."

"Can I come and watch?" asked Dickon, eagerly. "After midnight?"

Carl gave a nasty laugh and nudged Wilfred.

"What?" he said. "And mayhap get mistaken for one of *these* brats?"

Dickon turned pale underneath his grime.

"Oh—yea—I mean nay!"

"Begone then!" said Carl. "Before we put *thee* in chains!"

"That's one consolation anyway," muttered McGurk, when Dickon had gone and the men went to see to the four regular prisoners.

"What is?" asked Wanda.

"At least I won't be having *those* things stuck to my neck," said McGurk, with a shudder.

I got the impression that no torture the Terrible Twain could have devised would have scared McGurk more than those leeches.

For a short while we remained silent, listening to the men's hateful voices as they urged their prisoners to eat.

"Come on, Sir Geoffrey, this may be thy last meal!"

"Try this, Sir Irish Knight. 'Twill do thy soul good 'ere we hang thee!"

"Jerks!" muttered Wanda. "Two-bit, low-life, gloating jerks!"

Gareth and Gwyneth looked at her curiously, probably because of this outburst of very unmedieval language. But Wanda was past caring.

"*I* wish we had some gunpowder, too!" she said. "Though a few sticks of dynamite would be even better!"

"Hey, yes!" said McGurk, turning to the twins. "I was meaning to ask you. What do *you* guys know about gunpowder?"

Gareth smiled wanly.

"Guys and gunpowder," he said. "That is a brave jest, Sir Jack."

"Huh?" grunted McGurk.

"Guy Fawkes and the Gunpowder Plot," said Gareth.

McGurk looked astonished. So did we all, forgetting for the moment our terrible plight.

"So you know about *that*, too?" said McGurk, now very alert. "When *was* that, Officer Grieg?"

Wanda shrugged, still staring at Gareth in disbelief.

Gwyneth sighed and said, sadly, "Sixteen hundred and five."

Then she looked anxiously at her brother.

"Aye," he said. "We might as well tell them now. . . . We—we have traveled through time," he said. "From the year of our Lord, sixteen hundred and ten."

"And we suspect that you have, also," said Gwyneth.

"Though from a later date," Gareth added.

12 A New Ally

We were stunned. Absolutely. We stared at the twins.

McGurk was the first to recover.

"You're right. But"—he glanced at our walkie-talkies—"how did *you* get here?"

"We were both suffering from a sudden ague," said Gareth.

"That's like a feverish chill," I said to the others.

"Quiet, Officer Rockaway!" snapped McGurk. "Go on, Gareth."

"So our parents sent for Doctor Zee—"

"He was an alchemist," said Gwyneth. "He gave us a potion of rare herbs."

"And we became drowsy and fell asleep," said her brother. He shrugged. "And here we are."

"How long ago?" asked McGurk.

"Oh, more than a year," said Gareth. "We soon wore out our old clothes and they gave us these rags."

This was bad news to us. The full horror of our

plight was beginning to sink in. There seemed to be no chance of another sudden time switch now, back to the twentieth century and the good old U.S.A. With or without the black boxes.

And that meant no chance of a reprieve from what was in store for us after midnight.

"What time d'you—d'you think it might be?" asked Willie, proving that even he was thinking on similar lines.

"About nine o'clock," said Brains, glancing at the wrist which usually wore the watch he hadn't brought along. All he saw now was a rusty iron manacle. He shuddered.

"Another fifteen hours," said Mari. "But do not look so sad, Brains. A lot can happen in that time, can't it, Chief McGurk?"

"Sure," murmured McGurk, not looking any too happy, though.

He turned to the twins.

"This Doctor Zee," he said. "Do you think he'll be trying to bring you back to the—uh—seventeenth century?"

"Alas! We fear not," said Gwyneth.

"To undo the work of the potion, we would have to find another potion to counter it," said Gareth.

"We have tried all manner of herbs," said Gwyneth.

"At first we thought of asking Lord Lestrange to help," said Gareth.

"Why?" asked McGurk.

"Well," said Gareth, "we think he too may be an alchemist."

"Also," said his sister, "also he sometimes looks very like Doctor Zee."

"*Very* like," said Gareth.

There was silence for a while, broken only by the sound of the jailers' voices, still taunting the prisoners.

Then I couldn't resist it. I mean this was a chance in a lifetime, even though that lifetime had only a few more hours to run.

"Did you—did you ever see any of Shakespeare's plays?" I asked. "When they first came out?"

A sudden smile crossed both their faces.

"Aye! That we did!" said Gareth.

"We even saw Mr. Shakespeare acting in one," said Gwyneth. "*Julius Caesar.*"

"And he actually spoke to me in the interval," said Gareth, proudly.

"What did he say?" I asked, with bated breath, forgetful for a moment of all castles and wicked princesses and torture chambers.

Gareth grinned.

"He said, 'Here, boy, run and fetch me a mug of

ale—I am greatly in need of it. These filthy, lousy, beggarly, flap-eared knaves who call themselves actors—they are murdering my play!' "

McGurk had been gaping at us. Now he gave his chains an impatient rattle.

"What *is* this? English 101? Don't you realize our lives are at stake?" He glared at me, then Gareth. "Tell us about that secret passage. You say it starts down here?"

"We think so," said Gareth, looking very serious now. "You see, our house is—was—will be—only a few hundred paces from here."

"And this castle," said Gwyneth, "was—will be—"

"Just stick to 'was'!" said McGurk.

"Well, when we were in our correct century," she said, "the castle was in ruins."

"We used to play here," said Gareth. "Hide and Go Seek and such."

"That is how we came to find the passage," said Gwyneth. "Beyond the loose flagstone at the bottom of these steps. We—"

"Quiet!" whispered McGurk, as the jailers came back.

They started taunting us again.

"Saying your prayers, striplings?" sneered Wilfred.

"While you still have tongues?" jeered Carl.

"Tongues which—"

He broke off as another visitor arrived.

It was Piers, the armorer, looking very worried.

"I am come to see that the equipment is in good order for the morrow," he said, after giving us an uneasy glance.

"Ah, yes," said Wilfred. "Some of the spikes in the Helmet of Death need sharpening."

"And the threads on thumbscrews three and seven are wearing out," said Carl.

"And the gears on the rack tend to slip when bone-breaking point is reached," said Wilfred.

"Anything else?" asked Piers.

The men looked at each other, shaking their heads.

"Naught that we can name," said Wilfred.

"Well," said Piers, "you had better give every-thing a thorough double check. With eight souls to put to the test, other faults may arise. And then her highness would be angered indeed. . . . While you are doing that, I will examine this golden ribbon."

He came across and bent in front of Wanda.

"Oh?" said Carl, coming to join him.

"Yes," said Piers. "Princess Melisande wishes me to make twenty like it."

"I would rather 'twere thee, Master Armorer, than I," said Carl.

"Fie!" said Piers, straightening up and scowling at the fat jailer. " 'Twill not be difficult for a seasoned craftsman such as I. Now look you to *your* craft, both of you, and check those instruments."

When the men had gone into the torture chamber, the confident look left Piers's face. He stooped to the zipper again, sighing and shaking his head.

"You'll never make it!" said Brains.

"I made these chains and most of those instruments," said Piers.

"Maybe," said Brains, "but zippers require special tools and materials. You'll never make her *one*, never mind twenty."

To our surprise, Piers nodded sadly.

"I know," he said. "You are very right, young sir. Come the next full moon, I am a dead man. That is why I have brought your captain"—he fumbled inside his doublet and took a quick look at the doorway—"this."

It was a key. He handed it to McGurk.

"Quickly," he murmured, "conceal it on thy person. Let *them* not see it."

Something like joy began to shine out of McGurk's eyes.

"For the chains?" he whispered.

"Aye," said Piers. "Both wrists and feet."

"All of us?"

"Verily! I made them all with the same lock. Now all you will have to do is free yourselves and make haste to King Henry."

"Fat chance!" said Wanda, suddenly slumping. "What about the Terrible Twain?"

Piers shook his head.

"Nay, I cannot do everything."

"Leave *them* to me!" said Mari.

"Eh?" grunted McGurk, swivelling to get a better look at her.

"Have confidence in me, Chief McGurk," said Mari. "I think I know a way to put them out of action. One of them at least."

"And the other?" said Gareth, doubtfully.

"I think he will be weakened after I'm through with them," said Mari. "But we now have the key and there are eight of us."

"Just so!" said Piers, nodding eagerly. "As I had thought. And then?"

"We think we might be able to use a secret passage," said McGurk.

"Oh, so you have heard of that, too?" said Piers.

"Yes," said McGurk. "Have you?"

Piers nodded again.

" 'Tis rumored that it starts somewhere down here and leads out under the moat. Whither to, I know not."

"Does anyone else know?" asked McGurk, looking anxious.

"Nobody that I know who is still living," said Piers. "And I have kept it to myself, lest some day I might have dire need of such a bolt hole."

"If it exists," said Wanda.

"Aye," said Piers. "But what does it matter? Once you are free from your chains you will be able to release your magic boxes and use them to get out with."

"Oh . . . yeah . . . sure . . ." murmured McGurk, not looking very hopeful. "Well, thanks . . ."

"You can thank me by succeeding and telling the king of the plight of his son, Prince Geoffrey. Then he will come and slay Melisande the Bad and all her evil retainers and free the rest of us." Piers glanced at the doorway. "Now I must go and pretend to repair the torture equipment."

He went into the next chamber. We heard him talking with the men.

"Right," said McGurk to the twins. "Now tell us what *you* know about this secret passage."

Whether or not something of Shakespeare had rubbed off on Gareth, I don't know. But when he got down to it, he was pretty good with words, giving us a very clear description of the passage, its route—and the problem.

I made a diagram of the problem later, and here it is:

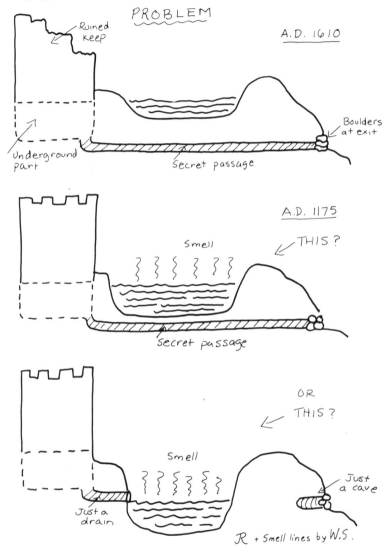

PROBLEM

Ruined Keep

A.D. 1610

Boulders at exit

Underground part

Secret passage

A.D. 1175

Smell

THIS?

Secret passage

OR

THIS?

Smell

Just a drain

Just a cave

R + Smell lines by W.S.

"The moat was shallower in the seventeenth century," said Gareth. "Not as deep and not as stinking."

"We have taken soundings," said Gwyneth. "Privily."

"So we think that between the twelfth and the seventeenth centuries it gradually became silted up," said Gareth.

"And that's the problem," said Gwyneth.

"Aye," said Gareth, sighing. "The passage leading *under* the moat in the seventeenth century might only lead *into* it now."

"Might only be a drain hole now," said Gwyneth.

"Oops!" exclaimed Willie, rattling the chains as he clutched his nose at the very thought.

"Are you sure?" McGurk asked the twins.

"Well, no . . ." said Gareth. "But—"

"It's a chance we have to take!" said McGurk. He looked around at us. "Men?"

"Sure," we murmured, some doubtfully, some eagerly.

"Good!" said McGurk. "Now it's up to you, Officer Yoshimura."

"You bet, Chief McGurk!" said Mari, looking like she was raring to put her plan into action. "Whenever you are ready!"

13 Escape?

About an hour later, after Piers had gone and the Terrible Twain were sitting at the table, taking turns to swig from the jug, Mari made her move.

Wilfred had just laid his arms on the table and his head on his arms, ready for a short nap. In fact a curious squealing snore was already escaping from his slit mouth behind the hood when Mari said, in the voice of Carl, "That is it! Snore like a stinking pig and set my teeth on edge, knave!"

Wilfred sat up with a start.

Carl had just lifted the jug to his lips, pulling up the hem of his hood to make way for it, and the sound of his own voice, seemingly coming from the jug, had shocked him into immobility.

"Who art *thou* calling a knave, knave?" demanded Wilfred, now fully awake.

"Not I!" said Carl, finding his own voice. Then he added, or *seemed* to add: "Thou long, lank, lousy, boss-eyed jackanapes!"

Now this was where the men's gloating cruelty in putting on hoods just to scare the prisoners rebounded on them. Because Mari had it made. With hoods covering their lip movements, it really did seem like each was saying the words she was putting into his mouth.

Wilfred leaped to his feet.

"Boss-eyed, am I? Jackanapes, eh?"

"But—but that was not I who spoke!"

"Did I not hear thee with mine own ears, *liar*?"

"Ho, liar am I?" roared Carl in his own voice. "Thou ditch-born, slit-mouthed dunderhead! . . . And take thy face away from mine. Thy breath stinks even through thy hood!"

Which was Carl's genuine voice and which was Mari's, I couldn't have said. But she told me later that the bad breath jibe was hers.

"There is nothing like personal truths to get someone mad," she explained.

At that point, she let Wilfred reply in his own words.

"My *breath*? Thy *whole body* stinketh as one who bathes but once a year—and then in the moat!"

Carl must have been stuttering with rage, the way his hood was wagging.

"Oh—oh *aye*?" he managed at last.

"Aye!" sneered Wilfred.

They glared at each other in silence, heads jutting forward, arms braced on the table.

They might have gone on like that for several

minutes, too. After all, these were men of action, not of words. But Mari helped them out and in so doing pepped up the dialogue again.

"Thy face is so foul that not a hair will grow on it!" she made Carl say.

"The hair on *thy* face," she made Wilfred reply, "is like unto a dirty dog's hair. The hair from beneath its tail!"

Carl twitched as if stung.

"*Thy* face is as bare as the backside of the hairless ape Lady Polly once owned," Mari made him say. "But even uglier!"

And that did it. In the next second, Wilfred's hands were at Carl's throat. And in the next second after that, Carl's knee was in Wilfred's groin.

Then they really got going, rolling on the floor, kicking, scratching, growling, snarling, swearing. During which time, McGurk had swiftly unlocked his own chains and had passed the key along.

"For this I will kill thee!" grunted Wilfred, grabbing a handful of Carl's beard through the hood, ready to slam the fat man's head against the stone floor.

" 'Twill take—more than thee—to do *that,* dog!" said Carl, jabbing at Wilfred's eyeholes with forked fingers.

And no, it wasn't Mari's voice this time. These were their own words as they rolled across the floor, panting and straining to get the upper hand. Mari was too busy unlocking herself by now, anyway.

Finally, Wilfred managed to grab Carl's beard again, and this time he made no mistake. He banged the other's head against the floor with a sickening thud. Carl's body instantly went still and silent.

Wilfred wasn't in too good a shape either. All he could manage was to get as far as his knees, before he bent over his partner.

"Thou asked for it!" he muttered. "Come on! Wake up! I did not hit thee that hard. I—"

But Carl didn't wake up and Wilfred never got any further, because just then eight newly freed prisoners jumped on him, flattening him against the floor.

Correction. *Seven* newly freed prisoners jumped on him. The eighth, Gareth, had grabbed the heavy earthenware jug.

"Leave the knave's head clear," he said. "And I will smash this on his skull."

I guess a whole year back in the twelfth century had made Gareth somewhat barbaric.

But McGurk had only spent a day there, and he was still his old civilized if rather bossy self.

"No!" he commanded. "Put it down. We're officers of the law, not murderers like them."

"But—" Gareth looked as if he were going to disobey. Then his sister plucked at his sleeve.

"No, Gareth," she said. "He is right. Anyway, the king will soon be taking care of *them*."

"Come on," said McGurk, from his seat on Wilfred's groaning head. "We're wasting time. Officer Bellingham, go bring us some of those hanging ropes from the torture chamber. You, too, Officer Yoshimura."

Five minutes later, the two men were trussed up like a couple of oven-ready turkeys and gagged with their own hoods.

"They shouldn't give us any more trouble now," murmured McGurk, his eyes gleaming with satisfaction. "Now let's get our black boxes released."

The wire cage didn't give us any problems and soon the walkie-talkies were strapped over our shoulders again.

Then: "What about the jailer's meals?" said Wanda. "Isn't someone likely to bring them food and find them here like this?"

McGurk's earlier satisfaction changed to worry.

"Gee, yes! Good question, Officer Grieg. I wish I knew the answer."

"Fear not," said Gareth, grinning. "These two are so feared and disliked by the kitchen staff that they have their own food supply down here. In some stinking lair beyond the cells."

"*That's* okay, then," said McGurk. "Now let's see if we can find the entrance to the passage."

"Hold it, McGurk," I said. "What are we going to do about the regular prisoners? Prince Geoffrey and The McGurk and the other two. Do we free *them* now?"

A cloud seemed to cross his face.

"No," he said reluctantly. "They're too weak. If we find the passage, it could be a struggle to get through it. Then there's the nine-mile walk."

I nodded. "So we leave *them* to be taken care of by the king, too?"

"That's all we can do," murmured McGurk, looking terribly anxious all at once.

I guess he was thinking again about what might happen to him if his great times thirty grandfather croaked without having children.

" 'Tis here, I think!" came Gareth's excited voice from out in the passageway at the foot of the stairs. "Behold!"

He was standing on one of the flagstones with his legs apart, rocking gently from side to side.

"Ah!" said Gwyneth. " 'Tis loose! That is just how we found it in the seventeenth century."

"Great!" said McGurk. "Now stand aside and let's see if we're *really* in luck!"

It didn't take him and Gareth long to lift the stone. A small avalanche of dirt fell away from its underside as they eased it away from the hole.

"Pass me that torch," said McGurk, on his knees,

peering into the blackness.

Wanda handed him the one she'd been holding and we all gathered around, taking care not to get our hair singed.

The hole was about four feet deep, lined with stones. At the bottom, we were thrilled to see another aperture branching off at right angles.

"It doesn't *look* wet," said Wanda. "With all these cobwebs, it doesn't *look* like it's been used to drain off floodwater."

"Not recently anyway," grunted McGurk. "Officer Sandowsky?"

Willie sniffed deeply.

"No," he said. "Maybe a bit of a damp earth smell."

"But no moat smell?" said McGurk.

"No," said Willie, sniffing again. "Not yet, anyway."

"Right, men," said McGurk. "We'll give it a whirl. Officer Grieg, bring another couple of torches— we'll need all the light we can get. Gareth, you take this one and lead the way. Take Officer Sandowsky, too, to monitor for any sudden moat smells."

"What about you, McGurk?" said Wanda, with a critical look in her eyes.

"I go last," he said. "If they *do* get wind of our escape and they *do* follow up in pursuit, I need to be the first to know."

"And also be the first to be caught," said Mari, anxiously. "Do you realize that, Chief McGurk?"

He smiled grimly.

"Sure," he said. "It comes with the command. But they'll have to kill me and chop me up in pieces to get past me in *that* narrow space."

Wanda bit her lip.

"Gosh, I—I never thought of it that way, Mc-Gurk!" she said.

"Yes, well, get going," he said. "Gareth and Willie are past the bend already."

It was dusty down there, and smoky from the torches, and not the best of environments for someone like me with a tendency to suffer from hay fever. But there *was* air down there, enough for the torches to keep alight in, so I wasn't too worried.

Brains wasn't sure, though.

"I hope there's no gas," he said, as he crawled in front of me.

"Gas?" said Wanda, from just behind me. "In the twelfth century?"

"Yes!" said Brains, sounding snappish. "*Marsh* gas. From the moat just above us. That can explode, too, you know, when exposed to naked flames."

"Thanks!" said Wanda, drily. "There's nothing like having a cheerful attitude!"

"Shut up, you two in front!" came McGurk's muf-fled voice. "There isn't all *that* much air. So don't use it up yacking!"

Well, it seemed to take hours, but finally the passage widened into a short cavern—a bit like the one I'd started in. And it, too, seemed to have-a large boulder or bunch of large rocks blocking the entrance, judging from the daylight that came through the cracks and chinks.

"We've done it!" cried Wanda, clapping her hands. "Queen Guinevere's bower!"

"Yeah!" grunted Willie, already peering through one of the cracks. "The only thing is . . ."

"What?" said McGurk, coming into the cavern just then.

"Tell 'em, Gareth," said Willie.

Gareth was standing close to another peephole.

"The sun," he said. Then he screwed his head around to get a look from a different angle. "Yes," he said. " 'Tis still high. Still early afternoon."

"So what?" said Wanda.

McGurk groaned. "So it means we'll have to wait here for *hours*!" he said. "Until it gets dark!"

"So the men on the walls don't see us," said Willie, for once way ahead of Wanda.

"We are right under their very noses here," said Gareth.

"And the hillside is bare," said Gwyneth. "With no cover for hundreds of yards."

"So we're stuck here for the next six or seven

hours," said Willie. "So let's hope they don't discover we're missing in the meantime."

"Oh, boy!" sighed Wanda, suddenly looking very squelched. "I'm sorry I asked!"

14 The King's Encampment

It was then that McGurk showed some of his best qualities as a leader.

Instead of having us sitting around, dithering and listening for signs of the alarm being raised, he got us busy working.

First, he had us remove one of the large stones that blocked the entrance.

"Just one, so there's more light," he said. "And more chance of hearing the men on the walls if the alarm is sounded."

Then he organized us into a human chain.

"There's plenty of broken rocks in here, men. I want them transported back into the passage."

"Why?" asked Wanda.

"To block it up at some point back there. Then if they do find the jailers before we're ready to go, they won't get very far."

"But won't they send men to this end?" Brains asked.

"I'm counting on them not knowing where it comes out," said McGurk. "You heard what Piers said. He's the only one who seems to know about it."

"*We* did," said Gwyneth. "Gareth and I."

"Yes, but only because you'd already found it in the seventeenth century," said McGurk.

Well, it was better than sitting on our hands. So we spent the best part of the waiting time passing back rocks for McGurk and Gareth to block the passage with.

McGurk had picked a point just under the moat—after getting Willie to sniff the cracks in the roof of the passageway.

"Why there?" said Wanda.

"Well, first because the light from the cave just about reaches this far, and it won't be long before the last torch is burned out," said McGurk. "And second, if they do follow us to that point and start digging around the blockage, they'll stand a good chance of knocking a hole in the bottom of the moat and drowning."

"Or dying of the smell!" said Willie.

It was such a good idea, I drew a plan of it later, and here it is:

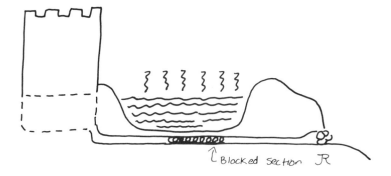

Blocked section JR

"Anyway," I said, "they'll probably be too scared to follow us when they find the black boxes have gone. They'll think it's some kind of magic."

"Correct, Officer Rockaway," said McGurk. "That's why I brought away the key, so they'll think we got out of those chains by magic, too."

"Oh?" said Brains.

"Yeah," said McGurk. "Like we said some magic words that shrunk us to the size of mice and let us slip through the cuffs and leg irons that way."

Gareth, knowing the medieval mind, agreed. But he wasn't all that far from having a medieval mind himself.

"What *are* those boxes, anyway?" he said.

"An example of late twentieth century technological advancement," Brains began. "They—"

McGurk cut him short.

"They let us talk at a distance," he said. "Without hollering. In fact you'll soon be seeing for yourself."

He bent over his walkie-talkie. "I'm setting mine to receive. Officer Grieg, you'll be in charge at this end, looking and listening for an alarm or for anyone snooping too near. Keep your set on transmit, so you can warn us."

Well, that precaution wasn't necessary, thank goodness. But when McGurk and Wanda put in test calls at either end, Gareth's eyes popped to hear Wanda's voice coming through McGurk's box.

" 'Tis indeed magic!" he whispered—while up at the other end Gwyneth's reaction was the same, according to Mari.

Anyway, by the time it started to get dark, we had blocked off a good stretch of the passage behind us.

"If we'd held off from bopping the jailers until it was nearer the time," said Brains, "we could have saved us all this work."

"Oh, sure!" said McGurk. "But we couldn't be certain of the time without your watch, could we, Officer Bellingham?" He frowned. "In fact if we ever do get back to our home century, we're gonna have lots of training sessions in judging the time without watches."

"Now see what you've done!" Wanda growled at Brains. "You and your big—"

"I think 'tis safe to leave now," said Gareth, who'd been peering out into the open. " 'Tis dark enough if we move very cautiously until we reach the trees."

"Maybe we should wait a little longer," said Willie.

"No," said Gareth. " 'Tis only about four hours to midnight and we have to travel three leagues to the king's encampment."

"Nine miles," said Brains. "That's only just over two miles an hour."

"Yes, but through wooded terrain," said Gareth, beginning to push carefully at one of the large rocks over the entrance. "And in the dark."

"And without being sure exactly where the king's camp is," I said.

"We will be able to tell by the large number of camp fires," said Gwyneth, giving her brother a hand with the rocks.

McGurk, who'd also started to help, suddenly stopped.

"Yeah, but only when we get close enough to *see* the fires," he said. "Suppose we go in the wrong direction before then?"

Then Wanda smiled, her teeth gleaming in the dusky light.

"That's where *my* expert skill comes in," she said. "Just leave it to me."

She was right. I don't think we'd have been able to make it without her.

By the time we reached the woods, it was getting pretty dark, despite a full moon that was just beginning to rise. And of course we couldn't see any fires at that level.

But when we came to the stream, dimly glinting and sort of whispering, Wanda chose the tallest tree she could find and climbed it. Up, up, up into the deeper darkness of the foliage. We waited, hearing only the swish of branches and rustle of leaves at first. Then her voice came floating down.

"I've spotted it. . . . I think. . . . Yes, a definite orange glow in the distance."

"Which way?" asked McGurk.

"Downstream," she replied.

Gareth nodded. "That will be it. In that direction lies the forest of Radnor, where it was said the king was hunting."

Wanda shinned up six or seven more trees that evening, reporting the glow to be getting brighter all the time. And eventually we made it—just around a bend in the river, where the forest opened up into a large clearing. We took a cautious closer peek from a screen of bushes.

There seemed to be numerous fires, and in their flickering light we caught glimpses of tents and stacks of weapons, with dim shapes of men here and there, most of them lying on the ground in front of the fires.

Then Gareth spotted a pennant over one of the tents, lazily flapping in the smoky air, and he'd just said triumphantly, "There! The king's colors—red and gold!"—when one of the dim shapes loomed up close and a hoarse voice said, "Hold! Who goes there?"

The tip of his sword was already at Gareth's throat.

15 The King

"We have escaped from the castle of Princess Melisande," said Gareth.

"Melisande the Bad," his sister added.

"So why do you come here?" asked the guard, still with his sword pointed at Gareth's throat.

I felt uneasy. He kept peering beyond the twins to where the rest of us were still in the shadows.

"We must see the king," said Gareth.

The guard grunted.

"*Must* is a king's word," he said. "Not a serf's . . . And who are these with you? Step forward!"

We did as he said. He stared at us, a bit bemused. I guess we'd have felt the same if a man-at-arms complete with ring mail and sword had tried to gate-crash the town's Fourth of July barbecue.

"His son, Prince Geoffrey, is being held a prisoner there," said McGurk.

"He's so weak he's likely to die any day now," said Wanda.

At the mention of Prince Geoffrey the man stiffened. When he heard of the prince's plight he put up his sword.

"Come with me," he said.

It must have been more than a clearing. It must have been open country at the edge of the forest. The camp fires seemed to stretch for miles in concentric rings, with tents and tethered horses enough for an army. Many of these tents carried the king's colors, so we kept thinking we'd arrived at *his* tent when we hadn't. At last, however, we came to a bigger one. The guard looked inside and said something in a low urgent voice. Then he beckoned us to go inside.

A gray-haired man with a thick gray mustache and short beard was sitting on the edge of a truckle bed, frowning up at us.

"What have we here?" he grunted.

"They say they have escaped from the castle of Princess Melisande, sire."

"Oh, *her!*" he said peevishly, as if he considered her to be no more than a minor nuisance.

"And that Prince Geoffrey is held prisoner in her deepest dungeon, sire."

He frowned at us and said, "Is this true?"

"Yes, your majesty," said Gareth, bowing low.

The man made an impatient clucking noise.

"I am *not* his majesty. I am William Marshall, his chief knight. How do I know this is true and you are not here to get free meals? Or worse?" His eyes narrowed craftily. "Tell me who else is at the castle?"

"Sir Boris the Bold," said Gareth.

"Ach!" The gray man spit on the rush-strewn floor. "That scoundrel!"

"And Lady Polly, called the Brown Vixen," said Gwyneth.

"And truly named!" said the man. "Who else?"

"Lord Merlin Lestrange," said Gareth.

"Hm! You seem to speak the truth," said the man, getting to his feet. "And you say Prince Geoffrey is in the dungeons? How do you know? He has been missing for a long time, but she has asked for no ransom."

"No, sir," said McGurk. "Because she's more interested in drinking Prince Geoffrey's blood."

"And the blood of the other three in there," I said. "The McGurk from Ireland is another of her prisoners."

"Forsooth!" said William Marshall. "I have heard that *he* has been missing for many years."

"Same reason, sir," said McGurk. "Royal blood. The royaler the better."

"Wait outside while I put on more clothing," the man said. "Then I will conduct you to the king."

So at last we got to see King Henry himself. And let me tell you, it wasn't easy getting to see the King of England. Even in a hunting camp. Even in the twelfth century. I'd been starting to feel we'd have stood as much chance getting to see the president at Camp David.

The royal tent was huge, with furs on the floor and rich-looking tapestries hung up to divide it into rooms. Otherwise there were few signs of great luxury. The king himself was *very* plain and homely seeming. In fact we didn't think it was the king, just the butler or something, until William Marshall bowed and addressed him as Your Majesty.

I mean, for starters, he wasn't very tall. And the clothes he was wearing looked like he'd been sleeping in them—which he probably had. But when you got closer there was something about him that shouted top quality. The creased and crumpled cloth of his tunic was dyed a deep purple and looked the very best that money could buy. So did his wrinkled hose. And the short cape he'd thrown over his shoulders was trimmed with what was obviously very rare and costly white fur.

But it was his features and manner that impressed me most. He, too, had reddish hair and—believe it or not!—freckles—so that for a moment there I wondered if this wasn't a general sign of leadership the world over and in all ages. But *his* eyes were gray, not green, and they seemed to see everything: our black boxes, our strange clothes, even McGurk's freckles. They weren't shifty eyes, either. They were just active. Never still.

And while he looked at our clothes and the black boxes so keenly, he never showed the least hint of surprise or awe or nosiness. He looked like a guy who'd seen everything and was just checking, as his gaze moved swiftly from one to another of us, silently examining this and that while his aide told him what we'd told *him*. I mean, in short, that King Henry II of England was one real class act.

"And they say that The M'Turk of Ireland is held captive there, too, your majesty."

"That's The Mc*Gurk*, sir," said McGurk.

"That's what I said!" grunted William Marshall.

"I thank you kindly," said the king, giving each of us a quick but grateful glance, missing no one. "I had been wondering where that young puppy Geoffrey had gotten to."

"So what is your wish, your majesty?" asked William Marshall.

"We free him of course," said the king. "We storm that castle and free him. We will put that she-devil to the death she deserves and I personally will cut off the head of that treacherous Boris." He seemed to be getting worked up. When he mentioned Sir Boris he did a little dance of rage. "Seize the son of the king, would he? Throw him into some stinking dungeon, eh? Feed his royal blood to that—that woman, forsooth! I will not only have his head, but I will tear off his beard and use it ever after to sweep the royal privy!"

"Yes, your majesty," said William Marshall. "I will draw up plans for storming the castle tomorrow—"

"You will draw up plans for storming the castle *before* the morrow. We will march on that den of devils now, as soon as I have donned my armor!" He went behind one of the hanging tapestries shouting, "Muster the men for immediate action!"

"Yes, your majesty," said William Marshall with the sigh of a man who has just seen a good night's sleep blow away from him. "You eight wait here," he said. "Methinks his majesty will wish to reward you."

After only about five minutes—during which we heard the chinking of mail and the king's rapid-fire stream of orders to whoever was helping him to dress—he emerged in his suit of ring mail and a coverall emblazoned with his gold and red colors, every inch of his five and a half feet a king. He was adjusting his sword belt and his gray eyes flashed as he looked around.

"Where is Sir William?"

"Here, sire!" said William Marshall, hurrying in. He was fully clad in mail himself now.

Outside, horns were being blown and there was the sound of men's voices and horses' hooves.

"May we come, too, your majesty?" said Gareth.

"No," said the king. "You all look too fatigued and

hungry. You have done enough. Stay here, rest and sup. I have already given my servants the order to serve you with the finest of meals here, in my tent."

Sure enough, a couple of sleepy-eyed pages were spreading a cloth over a trestle table in the corner.

"But—" Gareth began.

"Silence!" said the king, crisply rather than angrily. "I will see to thy rewards when I return. 'Twill not be long. I take castles such as hers before breakfast."

William Marshall sighed.

"He does, too!" he murmured, as the king darted back behind the tapestry to get his dagger.

It was a heartfelt sigh, as if the right-hand man had seen many a dawn break while busy fighting when he should have been nice and cosy, tucked up in bed. And I could sympathize with him. I know what it's like to be the right-hand man of a human powerhouse, believe me!

Ten minutes later, the king and most of his men had gone, and we were sitting at the table, tucking into the finest pie I have ever tasted, with succulent chunks of venison inside a crisp light crust.

"Good food!" said Willie, through a mouthful of it.

"The best!" said McGurk, as if *he'd* been the host.

Wanda was enjoying it, too, but she had to pause to yawn.

"He was right," she said. "I don't know about you guys but I *am* too tired to go chasing back there."

Even McGurk had to give a grunt of agreement. He yawned, too, then blinked and turned to Gareth and Gwyneth.

"Well," he said, "we rescued the—uh—dragon."

"Yes, and for that we are truly grateful," said Gareth.

"Aye!" said Gwyneth. "Eternally so."

"Oh, you helped a lot yourselves," said McGurk. "In fact, if you ever get time-switched to the late twentieth century, look us up. There's a place for you both in the McGurk Organization."

"Yeah!" murmured Wanda. "If ever any of *us* get time-switched back there!"

"Anyway," said McGurk, refusing to be cast down, "at least we did what we set out to do, men. Mission accomplished!"

Then all at once there came a crackling and sputtering from the six black boxes. It had Gareth and Gwyneth jumping to their feet, wide-eyed. We, too, were a bit shaken, until The Voice (and this time it wasn't Mari's, but the controller's) boomed out.

"You have just uttered the final magic words, Sir Jack McGurk! Thy mission *is*, well and truly, accomplished!"

And even before the last syllable had died out, everything and everyone became caught up in what seemed like a whirlwind of colors: red, gold, blue, green, silver, and gray—gray as the king's eyes—before fading to black.

It was a black so black it was even blacker than the beard of Sir Boris, or the black on the flag and in the heart of her highness the Princess Melisande. Yes, sir. It was *that* black.

16 The Key

When I came to, I was lying fully dressed on the bed with the walkie-talkie quietly hissing at my side.

It was my regular bed, back home. Dawn was beginning to break and I could tell where I was in the faint light.

And, sure. I know what some people will be thinking.

It was a dream, right?

Well, if it *was* a dream, it was one which we all shared. All six of us.

We checked later that morning (the twentieth century morning, following the night we'd gone to bed with our black boxes). And we'd all had exactly the same experience—except for me starting out in the dark cavern and them as frozen "statues" on the hill.

"I mean, I've either discovered a *time* machine or a *dream* machine!" said Brains. "One that makes a whole bunch of people have exactly the same dream at the same time!"

"Like you'd fed all those details into a computer," said Mari, "and the walkie-talkies transmitted them into our sleep?"

"Something like that," said Brains.

Wanda was frowning. "Whichever way it was, it's very remarkable."

"You're telling me!" said Brains.

Well, then we started taking sides; some saying dream machines, some saying time machines. Wanda, Brains, and Mari tended toward the dream theory, McGurk and Willie for time machines, with me neutral, not sure which.

To back up the dream theory, Wanda and the others began to point out how so many details seemed to be formed out of real-life details.

"Like Princess Melisande," said Wanda. "The more I think about it, the more she had the looks of Sandra Ennis."

The Organization's unfriendly neighborhood archenemy!

Well, it figured. They did look alike. Even the names.

MELISANDE.

SANDRA ENNIS.

"And Lady Polly," said Wanda. "Didn't it strike any of you that if she'd been dressed in jeans and a cotton shirt she'd be the twin of Lady Thumb?"

"The woman burglar we collared in *The Case of*

the Four Flying Fingers?" I said, for Mari's benefit. "Yes. Perhaps."

"And all those details we'd been studying for the class Age of Chivalry project," said Wanda.

There was something in that, too.

Then Mari threw in what seemed like the clincher.

"The king's chief man," she said. "Sir William Marshall. To me he looked rather like Patrolman Cassidy."

Our friendly local cop. Yes. We were all nodding now.

Even Willie had started to waver.

"Hey! Yeah!" he said. "That gray mustache!"

"You're right, Mari," said Wanda. "For the project, I copied this Marshall guy's face from a photograph of his tomb monument. Only last week. And the resemblance crossed my mind then!"

We all remembered that drawing. Here's a copy of her copy—just the head:

Even McGurk seemed a bit unsure then.

"Well, he *did* get my name wrong," he murmured. "Just like Patrolman Cassidy when he's kidding me."

"But that could have been a coincidence," I said. "Sir William wasn't kidding, I'm sure. Maybe his hearing isn't—wasn't—too good."

There was silence then for a minute or so. Brains broke it.

"I wonder how the king went on, rescuing the prisoners?"

"Oh, he managed okay," said McGurk. "No problem. I mean *I'm* here to prove it. And if he rescued my great-great- uh—my ancestor, he'd rescue the others."

"If he *was* your ancestor," said Wanda. "There must have been lots of other McGurks, you know."

"Yeah, but only one leader," said McGurk, as if that settled it. "My ancestor." He sighed dreamily. "If only we'd been able to stay another few hours, though. . . ."

"Why?" I asked.

"Well, when the king came back, after busting the castle, I bet he'd have rewarded us."

"Sure," said Wanda. "He said he was going to. Why? What d'you think he'd have done?"

"Knighted me, for starters," said McGurk.

Wanda sniffed and gave her hair a toss.

"Get him!" she said. "Rise, Sir Jack The McGurk!"

"What worries me," I said, "is what the king *did* do when he got back."

"What do you mean, Joey?" asked Mari.

"About Gareth and Gwyneth," I said. "I mean they're probably still there."

"Yeah," said Brains. "Being on a different time-switch system and all."

"Oh, they'll be okay," said McGurk. "They'll probably get our share of the reward."

"Well, he did seem to be a very fair-minded kind of man," said Wanda.

"Sure," said McGurk. "They helped save his son, didn't they? No problem. I bet he makes Gareth a page or a squire or something in his own court. And Gwyneth a lady-in-waiting."

"Well, I hope so," said Wanda, still looking concerned. "But I'd rather think they managed to get back to *their* home century."

We didn't know it at the time, but we were eventually to learn *exactly* what happened to Gareth and Gwyneth, and that they *did* get safely back to the seventeenth century, and . . . But that was still ahead of us. All we could do that morning was shrug our shoulders or cross our fingers and hope for the best.

Then, as I crossed *my* fingers, I remembered something that set me veering back to the dream theory.

"Hey! Lady Thumb!" I said.

"What about her?" said McGurk.

"The fancy word for thumb!" I said. "The one the doctor used when I broke mine. *Pollex!*"

That even had Willie wavering again.

But not McGurk. He was sticking to the time-travel theory and still does.

"Another coincidence," he said.

I was going to remind him how he was always telling us to look for the real explanations behind seeming coincidences. But he was barreling on.

"Here's something you can't explain away," he said, with a very bright gleam in his eyes. "Officer Grieg! Stand up and turn around!"

Looking puzzled, Wanda did this. She was wearing her pink windbreaker.

"See that?" said McGurk, pointing to her back. "*I* spotted it as soon as she arrived."

It was a faint red smear.

"Blood," said McGurk, as we peered at it and Wanda pulled at her windbreaker so she could see it, too. "Where the bird's head hit her when Bluebeard lopped it off."

"Well, it is very, very faint," said Mari.

"It could be jam," said Brains.

"Officer Sandowsky?" said McGurk.

Willie bent his nose to it.

"No," he said. "I don't get a whiff of *anything*."

That was strange in itself, I thought.

"Come on!" said Wanda. "I could have gotten it in the kitchen. Mom was making burgers yesterday."

Willie had another sniff.

"No," he said. "Definitely no beef."

"Okay," said McGurk, still with that gleam in his eyes. "Suit yourselves. But how about *this*?"

He stood up, leaving his chair rocking, and carefully turned one of his pockets inside out over the table.

We stared at the small heap of reddish dust he'd deposited there.

"Looks like rust to me," said Brains.

"Smells like it, too," said Willie, after bending over it.

"Okay, Officer Bellingham," said McGurk. "You can take some for analysis if you like. But you'll find it *is* rust."

"Why are you so sure?" asked Wanda. "And what if it is, anyway?"

"Because," said McGurk—and his eyes were glowing now, not just gleaming—"*this* is the key. The key for our manacles and leg irons. The one Piers gave me. The one that I put in this pocket when we escaped."

"But—but that was new," said Wanda. "Still shiny."

"I know," said McGurk. "But that was all of eight centuries ago. And remember what happened to Count Dracula's body when they finally nailed him. It crumbled to dust even as they looked. Just like it would have if he'd lain in his grave undisturbed all that time."

Well, that was enough to win Mari and Brains over to the time-travel theory. Even Wanda looked a lot less sure.

As for me—well, there *was* one other theory that could explain that rust.

But no.

It wouldn't be at all like McGurk to fake evidence. To scrape some rust off a bunch of old nails he'd found in the basement.

Or would it?

I tell you, I'm still in two minds. In two, three, or four minds.

But one thing is certain.

McGurk has never varied one jot from the time-travel theory.

"Anyway," he said that morning, while our heads were still reeling from that whammy of his. "What we've got to do now is add this latest achievement to our list."

He meant the list at the bottom of our notice on the door, giving all the cases we'd cracked. Like BANK ROBBERS BUSTED and so on.

"Any ideas, men?"

"Yes," I said. "I've already given it some thought. In fact I typed it already, before I came in."

I pulled the slip of paper out of my pocket. McGurk snatched at it and frowned as he read it.

```
Posterity Preserved
```

"What's *that* supposed to mean?" he said.

"Well—*you*," I said. "You're the posterity referred to. The descendant of The McGurk. And by saving him we saved you."

He softened up a little.

"Yeah . . ." he murmured.

He liked the idea, I could tell.

But then he announced what he said was an even better one.

"More in line with our mission," he said. "And *I've* written it down already, too. But I want Officer Yoshimura to copy it out in that fancy Old English lettering of hers. Okay, Officer Yoshimura?" he said, passing a scrap of paper across to her.

She looked at it, puzzled at first. Then her eyes lit up and she grinned.

"Sure thing, Chief McGurk!"

So now at the foot of the list of triumphs on our notice we have this:

Distressed Dragons

Delivered